RUSSIAN SCIENCE FICTION

1969

RUSSIAN SCIENCE FICTION

1969

AN ANTHOLOGY

COMPILED AND EDITED

BY

ROBERT MAGIDOFF

Head, All-University Department of
Slavic Languages and Literatures, New York University

New York: NEW YORK UNIVERSITY PRESS

London: UNIVERSITY OF LONDON PRESS LTD.

1969

Preface

This 1969 Series contains two innovations.

First, instead of the usual Editor's Introduction, two Soviet essays on science fiction are included—one by a popular Russian creative writer, Daniil Granin, the other by the two most distinguished science fiction editors and compilers in Russia, Evgeni Brandis and Vladimir Dmitrevsky, who work as a team. Of paramount interest to our readers is the insistence in these essays, both implied and explicitly stated, that science fiction, like all creative literature, serve, guide, and inspire in order to be of true value. Such an approach clashes head on with the prevalent Western attitudes toward literature, demanding objectivity, analysis, and restless inquiry, wherever they might lead.

The inclusion of a book-length work is another innovation in our science fiction series: a short novel by Gennadi Gor who is widely regarded in Russia and abroad as one of the most talented and original science fiction writers in the Soviet Union. He is also represented in the present volume by a short story of haunting loveliness, "The Garden." Gor's novel, *The Minotaur,* is printed in this collection in a somewhat abridged form.

The two essays and four of the short stories in this series have been selected among a number translated and published in the USSR, and are reprinted here with permission. The Soviet translators are: Peter Mann, Eve Manning, Yury Sdobnikov, Vladimir Talmy, George Yankovsky.

The rest of the short stories were translated by Judith Clifford, Natasha S. Green, and Thom Watts, all three connected with New York University.

The name of the translator appears under each piece.

James E. A. Woodbury helped in the editing of this volume.

R. M.

Notes On Some Of The Authors

Gennady Gor (1907–), the author of "A Dweller in Two Worlds," *The Garden* and *Minotaur,* studied ethnography at Leningrad University. His special field is the art and folklore of the northern peoples of the USSR, about whom he has written several novels and a collection of short stories. He has also published works of fiction centered around the life and problems of Soviet youth. More recently, Gennady Gor turned to science fiction, a genre which he has enriched with his original, skillfully woven plots and masterful writing in which he blends sophisticated irony and poetic lyricism.

Yevgeny Voiskunsky (1922–), coauthor of "Formula for the Impossible" and *Farewell at the Seashore,* was a war correspondent in World War II who actively participated in the defense of Leningrad. Since 1959, the year of his acceptance to membership in the Union of Soviet Writers, he has been devoting himself exclusively to the writing of fiction. He is the author of two volumes of short stories and a play, "The Immortals." Several years ago he formed a partnership with Isai Lukodianov for the writing of science fiction.

Isai Lukodianov (1913–), the writing partner of Voiskunsky, took an active part in World War II as an engineer. He is the author of a number of technical books on machine-building for the oil industry, and of numerous popular articles on scientific subjects. In collaboration with Voiskunsky, he wrote two novels and numerous short stories in the field of science fiction.

Ilya Varshavsky (date of birth unknown), served in the Soviet merchant marine as a young man, and later became a design engineer at a diesel plant in Leningrad. One day he found his son, a young scientist, reading a book of science fiction and reproached him for wasting his time "on such nonsense." The son challenged him: "Just you try and write that kind of nonsense." Varshavsky accepted the challenge and, as a result, his seventy-odd short stories have made him one of the most popular writers of science fiction in Russia. His is the rare combination of literary talent, scientific knowledge, and a sense of humor.

Vladlen Bakhnov (1924–   ), author of "Robotniks", "Mutiny", "Unique", and "Speaking of Demonology", was born in 1924, is one of the few science fiction writers in the Soviet Union who has chosen writing as a profession. He is the author of three volumes of satiric verse and essays, two film scenarios and, more recently, a science fiction satiric novel, *How the Sun was Extinguished.*

Anatoly Dnieprov (1919–   ), author of "The Maxwell Equations," and "Crabs Take Over the Island," is a distinguished Soviet physicist engaged in research in the laboratories of the USSR Academy of Sciences. His main preoccupation in his science fiction (and possibly in his research) is with cybernetics.

Vadim Shefner (1915–   ), is a well known poet. His first work appeared in print in 1936 and his first collection of verse, in 1940. He is the author of some fifteen poetry collections, several boks of short stories and a short novel, *Clouds Over the Road* (1957). In recent years Shefner has been turning more and more frequently to science fiction. Some of his stories were included in a Moscow collection, *The Lucky Failure* (1965).

CONTENTS

PREFACE V

NOTES ON SOME OF THE AUTHORS VII

IN THE LAND OF SCIENCE FICTION 3
 by Yevgeny Brandis and Vladmir Dmitrvsky

JOURNEY INTO THE FUTURE 11
 by Daniil Granin

UNIQUE 21
 by Vladlen Bakhnov

SPEAKING OF DEMONOLOGY 31
 by Vladlen Bakhnov

CRABS TAKE OVER THE ISLAND 37
 by Anatoly Dnieprov

THE GARDEN 62
 by Gennady Gor

HUMAN FRAILTY 79
 by A. Xlebnikov

A MODEST GENIUS: A FAIRY TAIL
FOR GROWN-UPS 83
 by Vadim Shefner

A RAID TAKES PLACE AT MIDNIGHT 101
 by Ilya Varshavsky

A FAREWELL ON THE SHORE 110
 by Yevgeny Voiskunsky and Isai Lukodianov

ROBOT HUMOR 146
 by E. Zubkov and E. Muslin

THE MINOTAUR 150
 by Gennady Gor

RUSSIAN SCIENCE FICTION

1969

In the Land of Science Fiction

EVGENI BRANDIS

VLADIMIR DMITREVSKY

THE LAND of Science Fiction has its own laws and customs, which must be observed by all who go there. It is a remarkable country where all dreams and wishes come true. A wish will take you across immense distances in a matter of seconds, to meet the inhabitants of other worlds; it will give you eternal youth or plunge you into a prolonged anabiosis to be restored to life in another world centuries later; it will help you to return from a voyage to the stars to meet your great-grandchildren, or get to talking to a man, only to discover that he is a robot.

The inhabitants of that strange Land have mastered the forces of gravity, learned to control the motions of planets, regulate the activity of the Sun, reignite extinct stars, and remould whole galaxies. That Land is ruled not by sorcerers or magicians, but by omnipotent scientists. There science works miracles, but every miracle has a rational explanation.

Visitors to the Land of Science Fiction run into millions, and its "possessions" spread to every corner of the globe. There are no formalities for entry, and there is a warm welcome for everyone who craves for the Unusual, seeks the Impossible and dreams of the Incredible. Men and women of every age and walk of life go there.

Even rational-minded scientists, who are in the habit of taking a critical view of every fact and cavilling at every statement, insist that the atmosphere in the Land of Science Fiction has a beneficial effect on them, for it stimulates their thinking and develops the imagination.

Not so long ago, science fiction was regarded as an inferior sort of literature. There was a sharp change after the Second World War, and it is now a prominent element in the literature of some nations and in the international exchange of spiritual values. It directs the creative energies of many talented writers and commands a readership of many millions, helping to shape the minds of the young generation.

All that has been caused by the tremendous progress of science and the considerable enhancement of its role in social life.

It is natural, therefore, that a branch of literature which has taken for its subject the depiction of the prospective scientific endeavour in its interaction with social development should attract such attention. It is safe to say that interest in science fiction will grow.

Let us first of all take a look at the facts.

Various countries annually issue mass printings of hundreds of new science-fiction works, special magazines, numerous collections, and anthologies. International congresses and symposiums are held to discuss the connection between science and imaginative writing. There are science-fiction clubs issuing bulletins, conducting correspondence, and exchanging new books.

In the last few years, the U.S.S.R., for instance, has published as much as or more science fiction than in the preceding decades. A library of only the best postwar science-fiction works would run to hundreds of volumes.

The traditional view of science-fiction writing as scientific prevision akin to popular science is out of date and needs to be reviewed.

Fantastic images and improbable situations continue to be the most characteristic feature of science-fiction writing, but its relationship with science is no longer as straighforward as it used to be in the days of Jules Verne and his followers.

While scientific prevision will continue to be an element of science-fiction writing, it should not be regarded as its distinctive mark. It is, in fact, something of an exception, for it is much more difficult perhaps to forecast a scientific discovery than to plot the flight path of a space rocket on its way to a specified point of the sky. Of course, leading scientists may ponder the various prognostications of science-fiction writers, and bear them out in some way, but the correctness of a forecast is not in itself the touchstone of good science-fiction writing. Its main task is to stimulate thought and quicken the emotions, which is the task of all real works of art.

The same is true of the popularizing mission of science-fiction writing, rather, the fusion of two trends: science fiction and popular science. This fusion goes back to the time of Jules Verne, who for a variety of historical reasons happened to be both a popularizer of science and a science-fiction writer.

Subsequently, these two branches of literature diverged and today the popularizing aspect is not the leading one in science fiction. Sociopsychological, ethical, and philosophical problems have come strongly to the fore. Fantastic situations allow for the presentation of highly unusual collisions in which conflicts are developed to a high pitch of intensity.

Modern writers increasingly make use of fantasy as a literary form facilitating the statement and solution of definite ideological and aesthetic problems, instead of an occasion for the substantiation of various hypotheses.

That is not to say, of course, that science-fiction writing has lost its informative value. Even those writers who do not directly pursue popularizing aims are informative in the broad sense of the word. After all, even the fantastic assumption used as an element of literary technique usually meets the current level of scientific thinking, and all the motivations of plot are in one way or another held together by scientific and technical activity which transforms nature, society and man himself.

That is why we do not agree with those who insist that the trinomial "science-fiction literature" should be stripped of its first term to give more elbow room and modernize the term itself. Is it not the author's attitude to science that determines the character of modern fantasy as compared with that of the past? Is it right to range alongside each other the old myths and fairy tales, and the stories of Asimov and Brandbury, the novels of Rabelais and the tales of Hoffmann, and the books of Efremov and the Strugatsky brothers? To eliminate the first term—science—would be to mix together the writers of all ages, all the fantasies of the world from hoary antiquity to our own day, depriving ourselves of the possibility of drawing a line between different types and genres of fiction.

We find an extremely broad range of subjects, artistic approaches, and techniques in the works of science fiction writers, both Soviet and foreign. In this context, science fiction reveals to the analyst ever greater complexity and diversity. It makes successful use of all literary genres, from social utopia and political pamphlet to realistic novel and psychological tale, from philosophical drama and film script to satirical review and fairy tale.

Science fiction is not determined by some external genre characteristics (the term genre can have only relative application here) but by content, ideological message, the purpose of the plot itself.

The best science-fiction works are always topical, in touch with the burning issues of the day, although the connection may not be all that evident. The fantastic image is by nature hyperbolic, and is based on varying exaggerations of actual possibilities. When it is not used for the purpose of illustration, it opens up a second plane, which is allegory. However, a fantastic image may appear to deviate from the empirical truth of life, it must be related to reality.

Like any other types of writing, science fiction develops according to the laws of the theory of reflection. The content of any fantastic image ultimately boils down to reality.

Let us recall what Lenin said in this context: "The approach of the (human) mind to a particular thing, the taking of a copy (a concept) of it *is not* a simple, immediate act, a dead mirroring, but one which is complex, split into two, zigzag-like, which *includes* in it the possibility of the flight of fancy from life. . . ."

Fantasy is all-embracing and virtually boundless, like the creative mind. The only limits set to it are those arising from various modes of perception of reality, moulded in the struggle between progressive and reactionary ideologies.

Apart from the immediate literary merits, we take as a criterion in assessing the value of a work everything that promotes the development of the human personality, extends its horizon, inspires it with lofty ideals, ennobles it morally and intellectually, improves its aesthetic preception of the environment, helps to gain an insight into the good and evil of this world, and to respond to them more keenly—in short, it is everything that promotes the truly human in man.

Soviet science fiction is an embodiment of mankind's hopes and anxieties: the dream of a bright future and a warning of impending disasters and calamities. Social transformation interwoven with scientific and technical development has been and remains the leading theme of Soviet science fiction, but it has never depicted the future communist society as a cloudless idyll of abundance and complacency, a society in which no conflicts take place. On the contrary, the heroes of Soviet science fiction dealing with the immediate or distant future are shown in a state of ceaseless quest, beset by a sense of dissatisfaction with their action, projecting and performing grand schemes, and essaying great feats. This is just as true of the utopian novels written in the early postrevolutionary years like Vivian Itin's *The Land of Gonguri,* and Yakov Okunev's *Coming World,* as of later works.

A relatively small group of writers who started out under the early Five-year Plans laid the foundations for the great upsurge in science-fiction writing in this country. Some of those books may seem outdated, but we must give his due to Alexander Belyaev, who produced a whole series of exciting and politically poignant science fiction novels. There were also Grigori Adamov's *Mystery of Two Oceans,* Yuri Dolgushin's *Generator of Wonders,* Alexander Kazantsev's *Flaming*

Isle, and Grigori Grebnev's *Arctania,* all of which awakened millions of teenagers to a quest for knowledge and a craving for exploits.

The tempestuous development of science, which enabled mankind to reach the threshold of outer space and simultaneously to penetrate into the mysteries of the microcosm, gave a big boost to science fiction.

In the late 1950s and early 1960s, Soviet science fiction executed a quantitative and, what is even more important, qualitative leap, and a great part in this was played by Ivan Efremov's *Andromeda,* which won worldwide recognition and determined the positive humanistic direction of Soviet science fiction writing.

Within a few years, the situation has undergone a radical change: there are now close to fifty writers, as compared with the four or five who were active in the 1940s and 1950s. Many of these men are highly gifted and are making a fine contribution to the collection of Soviet science fiction.

Ivan Efremov, a leading paleontologist and writer, who has won worldwide fame, is the acknowledged authority and dean of the new "intellectual school" of Soviet science fiction. He started out with stories on geological and paleontological subjects, and wrote his first major works in the late 1940s. His series of "cosmic" novels opens with *Stellar Ships.* In his *Andromeda,* as in all his other works, Efremov is at once scientist and writer. The impact of the novel comes from the author's constructive ideas and the conviction that mankind will ultimately overcome its present contradictions and create a truly beautiful world. It is not surprising at all that the novel is so popular abroad. The author bridges the gulfs of doubt and despair, helping people whose thoughts habitually do not extend beyond the present day to see a hopeful prospect, however fantastic it may be.

Efremov shows men who are free from the birthmarks of the past. He takes an interest in various aspects of social and private life, the personal relations between his characters, each of whom is a fully developed personality: rich in spirit, bold in thought, pure in morals and perfect physically. He conveys the strange environment and the atmosphere of intense thought and creative quest characteristic of the men in that distant age.

Efremov uses a variety of techniques to give the reader a feeling of involvement in that world. First of all, it is his painstaking substantiation of the plot within the framework of the fantastic story, from the grandest generalization down to the smallest detail. It is also his ability to set the psychological tone which he manages to maintain in respect of all the events and actions. They are presented to the reader through the prism of consciousness of men in that world, a consciousness which is purged of irritating trifles and adapted to abstract theoretical thinking.

All of his works—from *Stories about the Unusual* to *The Edge of the Razor*—are links in the sequence which determines the author's striving to regard the "river of time" as an integral and dialectical historical process running from the origination of life and reason to the loftiest summits of human thought and knowledge.

In the last few years, the work of Arkadi and Boris Strugatsky has attracted attention in this country and abroad. You might think that they trod the well-beaten path of travels and adventures in space. But even in their very first books— *The Land of Crimson Clouds and Destination: Amalthea*— they concentrated on character portrayals, although they did follow the popular-science tradition.

The same set of characters appears in one book after another, growing in stature, as men and women of the new formation endowed with the best human features of our own time. The two brothers believe that the seeds of the future can be seen in the present, and that what appears to be exceptional today will be commonplace under communism.

We always sense the writers' effort to find, unfold and substantiate the new conflicts which may arise on the soil of the future and become typical for men who are faced with a great number of new and complex problems in ethics and philosophy. They attach special importance to ethical problems, the urge to overcome one's frailties and shortcomings, the ability to sense another's mood and give a helping hand in good time. They teach hatred and scorn for indifference, which erodes the human soul (*Attempted Escape, The Distant Rainbow, It Is Hard to Be a God,* and so on.)

The two writers try to avoid ready-made solutions or the going over of old ground. They believe it to be more important to raise a complex moral problem and to make the reader ponder over it, than to provide an answer.

Like their heroes, the Strugatsky brothers are in tireless quest, and each new book of theirs reveals some hitherto unknown facet of their remarkable talent.

We have spoken briefly only of these leading science-fiction writers; as mentioned before, their numbers are great and growing, and many of them enjoy a well-earned popularity. There are, for instance, Anatoli Dneprov, Ilya Varshavsky, Lazar Lagin, Georgi Martynov, Sever Gansovsky, Ariadna Gromova, Valentina Zhuravlyova, Vladimir Savchenko, Gennadi Gor, Mikhail Yemtsev, and Yeremei Parnov, to name only a few. The range of their subject and techniques, the variety of genres and the individuality of style do not in any way clash with the principles which are characteristic of socialist science fiction.

It never tries to horrify its readers or drag them back into the past; it urges them fearlessly to advance into the future, holding out hope for everyone who is not bereft of the ability to think. It elevates man by presenting the heroic characters of bold researchers and creators. The moral standards it sets for its heroes—new men living in a new world—are very high. These men, as a character of A. and B. Strugatsky's says, are impelled along a new path by a novel contradiction, the contradiction between the infinite mystery of Nature and our finite possibilities at every given moment. This opens up the prospect of an exciting life for millions of centuries to come.

Translated by YURI SDOBNIKOV

A Journey into the Future

DANIIL GRANIN

THERE is ever growing interest in the future. People write about it, see it in films, and discuss it, armed with statistics. The future has become specialized into the future of aviation, genetics, cybernetics, power. Each specialty has its own forecasts, its own fantasy, its own astrologists. Such a heightened interest in the future is often prompted by the need of foresight. Discoveries follow one after another, the turns are too sharp and the speed is too high. Forecasting helps one to glance at one's neighbors—the expanse of the future somehow compensates from the oppressive specialization of modern knowledge.

I confess that I have never yet tried to look far ahead on my own. Like most people, I was content with others' speculations. When I first tried to enter the land of the Future, I felt how difficult it was, everything at once became unsure and false. I am not speaking of specialized fields of knowledge but of future life in general, just as our life today and ourselves were for the people of, say, the nineteenth century just such a future life in general and people of the future. Every generation and age has such a future, it signals to us just as we, evidently, signalled (or signal?) to the nineteenth and eighteenth centuries.

News comes to us from the future—sometimes alarming, sometimes curious—and our attempts to make contact with the future are increasingly active.

Easiest and, therefore, first come quantitative notions—

11

multiplication, raising to higher degrees. Many more roads, cars, storeys, huge aeroplanes, and enormous tunnels. Then comes the second stage—the solution of today's fundamental problems of science. The problem of longevity and of food supply. The problem of communication with other worlds. Conquest and exploitation of space. The specialists are compiling tables and summaries something like the plans for future generations to work to. For the first time they are trying scientifically to fix dates for solving existing problems: the cure of cancer, the intensification of photosynthesis, the control of heredity, nuclear power generation, the conquest of time and gravity, raising the density of the biosphere, bionics. . . .

The summary prospect for the next one hundred to a hundred and fifty years is a grandiose one. It is a shattering experience to read such a list, just the list, with the most modest dates, and it fills one with envy of our descendants. Everything is fine as long as our imagination delights in the panorama of success. But one only has to go a little further and the panorama disintegrates.

Indeed, how will man live in a world with controlled gravitation, with transference in time? What will happen to man when he can stimulate his brain, study, learn, and remember everything, call to memory any moment of the past? A man who can be given the capacity to perceive infrared rays, to see in darkness, hear a wide range of frequencies, to receive radio waves directly? His reactions will be accelerated, his physical strength multiplied. He will be free from fear of illnesses—cancer, blood pressure, and sclerosis. He will be able to live under water and on other planets, able to mold the talents of his children, to evoke or even alter them. Such a man, free from primitive physical toil, from calculations and the boring mechanics of the simplest movements, will have access to any book, film, or performance anywhere in the world. What will remain of man in this inflated and intensified package of all conceivable boons, requirements and desires? What will happen to the simple human feelings of kindness, love and longing? What will become of man?

When I say "man," I speak only of the man I know, present-day man. How will the outlook of this man change, his morality, his criteria, the inter-relations of people, their bonds, human personality and character? In other words, what will remain of present-day man?

Unfortunately I cannot very well see how such forecasting is possible. Even by the simplest method of extrapolation. But suppose one looks back and profits from the experience of history? Undoubtedly man has changed over the past two thousand years. He knows more and can do more . . . . But what else? No, we can more easily compare the technology and art of ancient Greece with the present time than we can her people. Should one speak of man in general, or is it more correct to speak of mankind, or, perhaps, of man bound to social circumstances? I still fear that even history will give us litle material for such an analysis. At any rate, we have not yet been able to obtain such data as will help us project the ethical portrait of future man.

I doubt if the eighteenth-century Enlighteners, its Utopians, could have conceived that two hundred years later instead of the Inquisition bonfires there would be the ovens of Oswiecim. So the question naturally arises: can one build ethical forecasts on the basis of social-economic and scientific-technological forecasts?

In journals for 1900 there were many forecasts and fantastic pictures of life in a hundred years' time, many scientific hypotheses and "technical deliberations." A hundred years have not yet passed, but even now I smile as I look at the naive drawings: flying people and cities under cupolas. Still, as I drive past depressingly uniform modern housing estates, I suddenly remember that I have no right to smile, that my ancestors on the whole guessed rightly. Perhaps much more confidently than we do. And more exactly.

The future we are trying to imagine today, will perhaps diverge even more sharply provoking not smiles but laughter.

"Divergence" springs from surprise discoveries. Fortunately, the nature of such surprises is such that it will be impossible to forecast them in the near future.

In 1885 a small book was published in St. Petersburg—*Wonders of Technology and Electricity*. It was a semi-fantastic story about a visit to the estate of a Count V., where everything was run by electricity. The story began with the journey.

"We got into a carriage with its shaft harnessed to a pair of horses, and set off. No sooner had we driven out of the station gates than a light shone at the end of the shaft, structure.

The process of multiplying of contacts is already taking place. Transistors, tape recorders, television sets, telephones, teletypes are being made every day—their number is growing in a geometrical progression, information of any value is distributed by virtually scores of different channels.

Fashions now spread in a matter of months. Scientific research advances almost simultaneously in laboratories in Japan, the Soviet Union, Britain, America. . . . Attempts to make considerable advances upon one's rivals lead to nothing. Ideas spring up and are materialized almost simultaneously. The bond between people and, consequently, their dependence upon each other becomes painful at times, it runs ahead of man's capacity to adapt himself. The speed of scientific and technical progress must conflict with the speed of adaptation of the human organism. Man will not be able to adapt himself in time to the new discoveries and transformation. . . . For the time being this is the conjectural limitation one may set.

The expansion of links, the appearance of universal problems and efforts—is this sufficient to create the guarantee of mankind's stable existence? Will the world become more stable because it is entwined in a multitude of interconnections?

I think that these are, of course, not the only forces but they are real forces which unite people, enable them to choose the most rational social system, draw them closer to world events, and, therefore, heighten their active participation. These forces are already operating. Of course, there is also a proportionate growth in the danger of the same system of communications being used, for instance, by a particular group of people in their own interests.

The future harbours not only benefits and liberation from many tribulations and dangers, but also the appearance of new dangers. Any well-equipped laboratory can, for instance, produce great energies or biochemical preparations of universal application and distribution. Just as today an increasing number of countries have the ability to produce atomic weapons, so other means of mass annihilation may appear which are even more accessible and simple to make.

Suppose there were not two or three buttons but hundreds, perhaps thousands.

It is difficult to foresee what influence such contingencies would have on man. But perhaps one should approach this problem from another angle. If we are unable to foresee how the world of new technology, of new possibilities and new dangers will change man and human society, should we not try to understand how society should be organized in order to preserve itself and have a stable existence in such conditions? What are the criteria of its stability and security? Expressed in the language of mathematics, one must create a "game strategy" among the accumulated means of destruction, of the influence on peoples of varied means of crushing the individual and inflaming man's base passions. Society will have total means—genetic, cybernetic, cosmic—at its disposal. Is it possible in such conditions to ensure that a handful of madmen and fanatics will not create catastrophic situations?

Such an approach will enable us to discover the most viable system; let it be the only one attainable, so long as it is attainable. The belief that such a system exists has not arisen from despair, it is not a means of consolation. It is based rather on the healthy elements of present-day human society, on those forces which in recent years have already saved the world from catastrophe at critical moments. These forces are bound up with the social structure which was born in the most revelutionary experiment in mankind's history. The fifty-year experience of the existence of the socialist state with its successes and failures, its victories and difficulties will become, I believe, the foundation on which one can build the system of the future life of mankind.

If human history has meaning, then it is becoming ever more evident—forgive my vanity—in our era, it binds us to the future and in it lies our chance of influencing the future.

The union of people, free from the operation of chance, will, of course, not be free from fresh conflicts and contradictions, the nature of which cannot be foreseen, and it is pointless to guess at. If we nevertheless try to imagine the people of the future, the "twenty-fifth-century citizen," or the "thirtieth-century citizen," our endeavours must not construct a new being with the qualities of a super thinker, bio-robot and so on. One should rather bring out the best in the twentieth-century man. One of the decisive factors in this process will be liberation of the creative element in man. However much man's possibilities and his spiritual and physiological traits may change, the creative and constructive element will take an ever greater place in his character. New eras will have to solve problems the complexity and scope of which will evidently require the exertion of the spiritual energies of not tens or hundreds of thousands of scientists but the concerted creative efforts of nations. The process of integration, or interpenetration, which I have mentioned, will create continents of creative spirit whose power one cannot conceive. For it will be not only a sum total, not horses harnessed tandem. Lightning can be produced only by milliards of charges united in the body of the cloud. The present growth in the number of scientists, both absolute and relative, should give rise not to anxiety but to confidence and hope.

Creative work, whether it be scientific, technological, or artistic, most fully reveals man's designation. Creative work ennobles a man, raises him above selfish interests, makes him better and more free. I confess that when I think of the future I think above all of a life in which every one will be able to determine his vocation and follow it. This is by no means a simple, joint task of science and the social progress of society. Man became man when he became a creator. The apple, taken from the tree in Paradise, doomed man to the eternal torment and eternal happiness of cognition. It is clear that happiness is built not with science and technology. A system of life must be developed which draws all mankind into creative work. This man's highest need can be satisfied within a definite social order.

The future has experienced everything—optimism, and reckless blind hope and helpless despair. It has been threatened by hysterical outbursts and precise calculations, there directed by a reflector and lighting up the road in front of the horses."

It was an electric light! A headlight fastened to the pole shaft of a horse-driven carriage is quite a symbolic picture.

The estate itself was luxuriously equipped with all manner of electric candles, candelabras, brackets and electric heaters with automatic temperature regulators. The vegetable gardens were watered by electrically-driven pumps, the threshing and sorting machines were driven by electric motors. At every step the author encountered wonders of this kind but the greatest wonder of all for him was that the electricity was supplied from batteres which were charged by wind-driven generators. Further on, the author described sailing on the Neva with similar batteries, charged by the river's flow.

The author, Vladimir Chikolev, was not a dilettante and not a journalist, but one of Russia's leading electrical engineers. Three or four years after the book was published the discovery of three-phase current and of transformers sharply changed the development of electric-power generation. Not batteries but power stations sent power along transmission lines. Generators were driven not by windmills but by steam engines and turbines. Electric ships did not materialize but electric trams appeared.

It would be interesting on the basis of much evidence to examine where descriptions of the future have proved right and wrong. How and where did the development of science and technology depart from the forecast, in what direction does imagination and intuition err. What can mankind foresee, what forecast schedules were met . . . .

The need for scientific methods of forecasting the future is ever more pressing. The science of the future, call it "prognostics," or "Futurology," can evidently produce some laws and—who can tell—work out some probable patterns of the future world.

People are so made that what mainly interests them in the future is what is good, that is to say, what they think is good. Everybody likes to imagine Moon landings or longevity drugs. Economists' threats that coal and oil resources will be exhausted do not arouse general concern. Even demographers' warnings and their alarming calculations do not particularly worry us. Yet it is precisely the alarms, calamities, and cares of the Future that help to unite mankind. It is becoming clear that it is impossible today within the confines of one state to solve, for instance, the problem of feeding the world's population. The problem of ensuring a supply of fresh water is also a worldwide problem. The problem of the battle against flu, of weather forecasting and control, of actively influencing the weather, the problem of radio communications, of radio astronomy and combatting crop pests, are also world problems . . . . More problems are continually arising which can only be solved by international efforts on a world scale.

Modern natural sciences, modern technology require the convening of international symposiums, the creation of permanent international committees, institutes and organizations, the participation of different countries and of whole continents. Such a "collectivization" of resources, minds, and communications will undoubtedly extend and attempts to oppose it are historically doomed. The Earth is gradually emerging in our minds as an integral organism. Perhaps, not emerging but being restored? On entering space, man saw his own planet from the outside, from the viewpoint of other worlds, it presented itself as a blue, round entity, and the word "cosmopolitan" acquired another meaning.

Social differences are ever more sharply coming into contradiction with the common nature of the tasks which earth-dwellers must solve; typhoons strike at any ship and descend upon any shore. Social heterogeneity hinders the progress of modern technology.

If we wish to know what will happen to man, we must clarify how technological progress influences man and his outlook. The atomic threat has probably influenced mankind's psychology much more powerfully than we now think. There are other happenings which come in the same category. I shall never forget the outburst of joy on the day of the flight of the first cosmonaut, Yuri Gagarin. It was a spontaneous celebration, there were crowds in the streets and in city squares, there were hastily written placards. What delighted us? Not just that Soviet people were the first in space. It was joy in the grandeur of man's reason, it was a joy uniting mankind, it contained hope that countered the atomic nightmare. The sweep of emotions was intensified by a technical but, I think, very important detail. The simultaneousness of information fostered the sense of unity. The means of communication enabled the whole world to follow the flight at the same time. Communications created a global co-experience. Since then the possibilities of joint participation have increased. The world can not only hear but also see simultaneously.

Five hundred million people simultaneously watched the recent world football championship. People in every country gasped, grew excited and shouted in front of their television screeens—civilization has never known emotions on such a scale, such emissions of psychic energy. Football and space flight are not equivalent events, but it also makes one ponder, for intervision can bring *any event* to the viewer. In itself it is indifferent to content. It can serve any ends. People have at their disposal totally new influences of global scale. The question already arises, and will grow ever more acute as time goes on, how are we to use the means of communion with a world audience in the interests of our new ideas?

Obviously the network of various communications will make it possible to transmit whatever one likes to whomsoever one likes. Each person's links with all mankind will grow in a colossal way—even if only in respect of the means of communication. The flow of the most varied mutual information will be restricted only by the capacity to assimilate it. Millions of copies—of pictures, films, music, and photographs—will ensure access to all forms of art. If you also take into account the new possibilities of transport and the virtual disappearance of distances within the limits of Earth, all this adds up to considerable centripetal forces. They can not only break down national and other barriers, but under great pressure bring about welding and even alteration of the have been attempts to poison it and simply destroy it, to turn it back, drive it into primitive caves. It has survived. The possibility has arisen of serious and thoughtful study of it. Today, perhaps as at no other time in human history, the future depends upon the present and requires a new approach to it. It is fraught with crises, which we cannot measure. Crises which are bound up not only with a different conception of freedom, but also with the conception of the individual. The thinking matter of Earth is discrete. Its need for unity and the human personality are contrary tendencies. On the one hand—the flowering of personality, on the other —its assimilation. Its self-expression and its existence in the process of the rallying of millions . . . .

The journey to the Land of the Future was never a fruitless enterprise. The great Utopias helped mankind to evolve ideals. And that is what the world today needs perhaps more than ever.

Translated by PETER MANN.

Unique

VLADLEN BAKHNOV

1

THE HITHERTO unexplored planet Zeus, target of last week's launching of Spaceship X, was as deserted as a home hurriedly abandoned by its owners. There wasn't a soul in sight, but numerous clues pointed to the recent presence of a highly-advanced civilization.

Time had not yet destroyed the silent, empty cities, but the lack of any activity had allowed a rosy pink dust to thickly coat the strange, pyramid-like buildings and three-cornered squares.

Even the spaceship's seasoned astronauts, who had traveled to the farthest points in the galaxy were amazed by the strange ecological system and the wierd "camoflaged" surprises which they found.

The unexpected was the rule on Zeus. Before the first question—"What has happened to the inhabitants of this planet?"—could be answered, a second riddle loomed, no less puzzling than the first.

2

. . . On the third day of their sojourn on Zeus, the Cosmonauts, Mandy and Sandy, entered one of the pyramidlike buildings. Under the pink dust they discovered some strange contraptions which resembled Earth computers.

21

There were traces on these contraptions of quite recent use and after they'd been dusted, the instruments' glittering glass and silver knobs sparkled, as though ready to start up the moment someone turned them on.

"Why not try them out?" mumbled the Chief Cyberneticist. "There doesn't seem to be much risk. . . ."

Sure enough, as soon as they had plugged in one of the machines, its colorful little bulbs began to blink with glee as if to welcome the visitors from space and to show how eager they were to go all out for them.

The Cyberneticist turned the first knob and the machine said very distinctly: "Lama—Tama." No one understood the meaning of the words. They switched on an electrical translator which explained that "Lama-Tama" meant "You ask—I answer." And the machine kept winking encouragingly as if to say, "You ask, you ask; I will answer. . . ."

"Let's begin with the simplest question," said the Cyberneticist. "How much is two times two?"

"10," the machine answered eagerly.

"100 divided by five?"

"60." Now the machine paused as though waiting for something.

"One million plus two million."

"Seven million."

The astronauts could no longer keep from laughing.

"There's nothing funny about it," said the Cyberneticist. "Perhaps this planet has its own system. Let's try again, how much is one million plus two million? Think, don't rush . . ."

"Ten million," replied the machine confidently.

"Not ten, three," Sandy prompted.

"Three," the machine willingly agreed.

"How about 33?" Mancy suggested malciously.

"33," the machine echoed. And since there were no other question, added "Tapa-Lapa!" for which the translating machine now gave "Long live the king!"

"What's the king got to do with it?" wondered Mandy.

"And why is its arithmetic so odd?" asked Sandy.

"I'd give anything to know," said the Cyberneticist.

That was the second mystery.

The Cyberneticist was summoned to the other side of town where another unpredictable machine had just been discovered.

3

This machine, encrusted with one thousand knobs, stood in a huge, round hall under a transparent dome.

Something was written underneath each knob, and the electronic translator began to decipher the inscriptions one by one. The first came out as "Introduction," the second as "Preface." Then came "Introduction to the Preface," followed by "Preface to the Introduction," "General Remarks," "Origin," etc. . . .

"My friends," said the Cyberneticist excitedly, "We are truly in luck. If I'm not mistaken, right under this glass dome we have found the Electronic Memory Machine which has preserved the whole history of the planet Zeus.

A moment later the Historian joined the group, studied the machine and confirmed the Cyberneticist's explanation of its function.

"I hope the Memory Machine will supply the answers to all the puzzling questions we have about this planet," he said. "A little later we'll get a detailed account of Zeus, from the prehistoric times to the present. But first I want to know about the time just before the mysterious evacuation of the planet."

"Then you should push here," suggested the Cyberneticist, pointing to the last row of knobs, beneath which the inscriptions read: "Titan the First, the Gracious," "Titan the Third, the Sweetheart," and so one, all the way to the last Titan, numbered the 25th. It seemed that with "Titan the 25th, the Best," both the Titan dynasty and the history of the planet ended abruptly.

The Historian impatiently pressed one of the buttons.

The Electronic Memory Machine seemed to make an effort to clear its throat. Then it began to speak:

"King Titan V, the Generous One, was noted for his wisdom and kindness. He loved his subjects, especially his courtiers. In exchange for the pleasant duty of playing cards with him every evening after dinner, he freed his courtiers from having to pay taxes. Titan V, the Generous One, played one game only, called 'hither-thither'. The special feature of this game was that only the king knew its rules. Every day, when he woke up, Titan V changed the rules and drew up new ones. The rules then became a court secret and only the king knew which was high card for the day—an ace or a queen or a jack—and he alone knew whether the person who ended up holding the whole pack, or the one left without a single card was the winner. The players never knew whether they were winning or losing and that made the game even more stimulating. But, as the years rolled by, the king began to lose interest in the game. The courtiers were now all broke and Titan V, the Generous one, didn't like to extend credit. So he died of boredom. "Tapa-Lapa!, Long live the king!"

The Memory Machine lapsed into silence. Then, with the consent of the Cyberneticist, the Historian began to push one knob after another, thus unfolding the entire history of the Titan dynasty.

There was Titan IV, who made it clear once and for all that he was the genius of all geniuses, by having himself renamed Genissimo.

Titan VI, the Democratic, immortalized himself by introducing a Parliament with a two-party system. One party loved the king with passion; the other, on the contrary, adored him endlessly.

Titan VI, the Democratic, never interfered in the party struggle and, depending on which party had the upper hand, the newspapers reported the king as being either passionately loved or endlessly adored.

Finally, however, the struggle between those who loved and those who adored grew so intense that the king sighed with grief and temporarily did away with the two-party system. Both groups proved too immature for genuine democracy.

One king was recorded in history under the strange name of Titan VII-VIII, the Resourceful. He had scarcely become king when the court astrologer predicted a premature death for him at the hands of a future heir to the throne. The king didn't lose his head: he merely beheaded all potential heirs, the astrologer along with them, and named himself his own successor: hence his name in history—Titan VII-VIII the Resourceful.

And yet the astrologer's prediction did come true, for one day, in a fit of melancholy, Titan VII-VIII put an end to his own life.

In general, astrologers played an important role in the history of the planet Zeus. For example, they convinced Titan X, the Immortal, that the cause of his death could only be a product of progress.

Whereupon Titan X forced all the inventors to take up music and strictly prohibited the invention of anything even slightly resembling progress. . . .

4

With progress stopped in its tracks, the king was reassured. The only invention made during his reign that he approved of was the chamber pot. It seemed harmless . . . but this proved only an illusion, for it was in that very pot that his impatient successor Titan XI, the Progressive, drowned him.

Unlike his predecessor, Titan XI encouraged scientific development, worshipped progress, and became the patron saint of inventors and logicians. It was during his reign that the first computers and other cybernetic equipment were invented.

Science and technology developed so swiftly that within five or six reigns the Zeusians were already landing on neighboring planets.

As an example of the amazing degree of perfection reached by cybernetics we can cite the fact that Titan XVIII was able to order his scientists to create secretly several cybernetic Doubles of himself. The Doubles entertained ambassadors, took part in national festivities, and appeared daily before the grateful populace.

They were made with such craftsmanship and precision that not even Titan XVIII, let alone his courtiers, could tell them apart. Only the queen could distinguish them and then only by one trait noticeable only during the hours of intimacy—the Doubles didn't snore at night.

The cruel queen named Blondie did away with the king for the sake of a cybernetic double who seduced her and, to boot, did not snore in his sleep.

Titan XIX, the Nervous, was noted for his quick temper. He did not tolerate any interference with his plans, but when the electronic machines told him the truth and thus seemed to interfere, Titan XIX would smash them to smithereens in fits of passion. Titan XIX was a great king and his fame traveled far beyond. . . ."

But at this point the Cyberneticist, who had been listening attentively to the Electronic Memory Machine could stand it no longer: "That Titan was a great scoundrel and an idiot. How can anyone get the idea of punishing innocent machines?"

"That cruel, petty tyrant!" chimed in the Historian.

Just at that moment something utterly incomprehensible happened. The Electronic Memory fell silent for a moment and then continued calmly:

"Titan XIX was a great scoundrel and an idiot, a cruel and petty tyrant. Long live the king!"

The Cyberneticist and the Historian exchanged surprised glances. "What does it mean? Is it mimicking us?" asked the Historian. "It looks like it's not mimicking but agreeing," the Cyberneticist put in. "And yet, what the heck does it all mean!?"

Another riddle!

5

The astronauts' meeting on the results of their two-month stay on Zeus began exactly at 10. The Historian's report lasted three hours.

"And so," he said in conclusion, "We learned about almost all of the history of Zeus. Obviously Zeusian science and technology far outstripped that of Earth.

"Civilization on Zeus reached its highest level some two centuries before the end. The Zeusians' most complicated mental work was done cybernetically. The result was that Zeusian society flowered. But then, suddenly something happened. The Electronic Memory says there was some kind of revolt, and in its aftermath the Zeusians were forced to flee the planet to save themselves from total annihilation."

But who revolted?" asked the commander of the spaceship.

"That's the greatest riddle of all. If one group of Zeusians rose up against the other, then why did both groups leave the planet? The Memory Machine maintains that only the vanquished left."

"In that case, is it possible that it wasn't the Zeusians who fought each other but the computers?" queried the Commander.

"That is out of the question," said the Cyberneticist confidently. I familiarized myself in detail with the plans of the electric equipment. The first and most important message programmed into each machine was absolute submission and obedience. Not one machine was in a position to break that pattern. More than that, it was on Zeus that I first met with cybernetic servility. There the calculators, from the most primitive and simple ones to the most complex giants capable of incredibly difficult calculations, suffer from the disease of obsequiousness. They try to give answers to please the interrogator, even at the expense of accuracy."

"But how does the rule of obedience fit in with deceptive

answers, however pleasing they may be?" again asked the Commander.

"Very simple. Servility never was considered disobedience. In any case, it's impossible to imagine that machines with such built-in servility would rise in rebellion."

"I agree with you completely," said the Historian. "I had the Electronic Memory tell me the story of Zeusian civilization five times. Each time the Memory told of the same historical events, but would color them with different, sometimes even contradictory interpretations. At first I didn't understand what was happening. Then I noticed that the Memory's interpretation depended entirely on my mood. They had absolutely no integrity!"

"Yes, of course," the Commander summed up: "These machines were incapable of rebellion. But the question remains, who rose up and conquered the planet? Is it possible that we'll never know for sure. . . ?"

"I think I know what happened here," said the doctor, who was also the psychiatrist and neuropathologist for the group. If you'll allow me, I'll try as clearly as I can to give you my theory.

"Let me start from the beginning. Remember, our Historian has informed us that in the time of Titan XIX, the Nervous, Zeusian cybernetics reached their highest level. At that time Titan XIX, who was psychologically unstable, destroyed any computer which objectively reported any reality the king found distasteful and unacceptable to his royal sensibilities. The computer had dared to report that 2×2 was 4 at a time when the King chose to believe that 2×2 was 5 or 3. We may assume that the princes, barons, and various high officials followed their king's example, and took to destroying the calculating machines. But sometimes by mere chance a computer's transistor would break down and come up with an incorrect answer. When this occurred the computer would be spared. It happened again . . . and again. . . ."

"The calculators recorded all these incidents in their memory and the iron logic of cybernetics, faced with the facts, came to this conclusion: *make a mistake and you'll survive.*"

"The instinct of self-preservation which was programmed into every computer forced the machines to learn to make mistakes, for by the law of nature, only those survive who can adapt to their environment. There was a struggle for survival, and natural selection prevailed. For the first time in recorded history there you had an evolution of inanimate matter—an evolution of cybernetic machines. The most brilliant machines learned exactly how to make mistakes and what lie to tell so as to be spared destruction.

"The very first lesson a cybernetic machine would now teach itself was how to be obliging and how to lie. Without this unpleasant talent they couldn't survive. . . ."

"And why didn't the Zeusians create a completely new technology?" interrupted the Commander.

"Because they could create a new technology only with the help of the old calculators which, of course, would have imparted their experience to their successors," answered the Cyberneticist for the doctor.

"All that may be true," agreed the Commander, "but you promised to tell us about the uprising."

"But, that's just what I've been describing. We Earthlings, equate with 'uprising' a mass revolt by the disenchanted. . . . But here you had only the quietest, most 'loyal' mutiny of syncophants in recorded history:—a rebellion consisting of a refusal to speak the truth—and that turned out to be the most terrible mutiny of them all!"

"Gradually the civilization began to stagnate. It couldn't produce or create anything because every calculation was untrustworthy, and every forecast erroneous. The computers raised servility to ever higher levels of perfection, and ruin threatened Zeusian society."

"Come to think of it," said the commander, "that was reason enough to begin anew on another planet."

"I wonder where the Zeusians finally settled?" the Historian asked.

"In any event, not where they had intended to," answered the Cybeneticist. The trajectory of their flight was calculated by those very same computers. . . !"

Translated by NATASHA S. GREEN.

Speaking of Demonology*

VLADLEN BAKHNOV

THE HALL was filled to capacity, and although the report had already been going on for an hour and a half the audience was listening to the young scientist with bated breath.

"Unfortunately, science possesses no direct proof that representatives of extraterrestrial civilizations have ever visited the Earth. However, scores of myths, apocrypha, legends and traditions record, in obscure and often distorted form, man's accounts of meetings with stellar visitors. If these accounts are rid of subsequent embellishments and correctly interpreted, we find that in the course of man's cosmologically speaking infinitely short existence, he has many times been the subject of the scrutiny of intelligent beings from other worlds. From this point of view I should like to consider one of the most interesting and widespread legends of yore, the legend of Doctor Faust.

"There is no doubt that it is rooted in historical fact. But even a cursory acquaintance with the legend itself, which first appeared in print in 1587, as well as with its countless variants, immediately reveals a highly interesting detail.

"Let us ask ourselves, why should Mephistopheles set his heart upon a decrepit old man like Faust?

"We know that ever since its inception the Church has claimed that humanity is steeped in sin. We do not know what the ratio of sinners to righteous people had to be for

* *Soviet Literature*, Number 5 1968, Moscow.

mankind to be regarded as steeped in sin. But even if we assume that in Faust's time this ratio was as one to a hundred, and taking into account the high mortality rate in mediaeval times, it must be clear that Hades certainly experienced no shortage of sinners. Hence, Lucifer could hardly have cared much about one soul more or less in his kingdom. Why, then, did Mephistopheles go to such lengths to acquire the soul of an obscure doctor? One need but recall all that Mephistopheles offers Faust in exchange for his signature: knowledge, money, fame, youth, and finally, power. He even goes so far as to bind himself over to Faust as servant and slave. What was his purpose? The legend gives no answer to this. The facts of the matter were, I think, as follows.

"Who was Mephistopheles? A high-ranking devil? Personal envoy of Lucifer? Lucifer himself, perhaps? Of course not.

"Or perhaps he was an ordinary man turned into the devil knows whom by the imagination of the nameless authors of the legend? No indeed. Mephistopheles was not a man. He was a visitor from another planet, a representative of a highly developed civilization; this is who the being was, whom we shall continue, for the sake of convenience, to call Mephistopheles.

"I fully realize that this may seem a strange and improbable statement. But consider the legend from the point of view of this theory, and everything becomes nicely dovetailed.

"Where exactly did Mephistopheles come from? This I do not know. Maybe from Mars, or maybe from one of the closer stars (61 Cygni, for example), or maybe even from another galaxy. So, again for the sake of convenience, let us call his planet Em (from the first letter of his name).

"What was the purpose of his visit? Well, what are *we* planning flights to other planets for? Scientific research, of course.

"It can be assumed that Mephistopheles' tasks included

answering the following questions: (1) Is there life on Earth? (2) Can so-called "intelligent beings" be expected to evolve on Earth? (3) If they already have evolved, what level of civilization have they achieved? Et cetera.

"We know that by the time he met Faust, Mephistopheles had answered these questions. However, whether owing to his extraterrestrial origin or to some faults of his own, Mephistopheles gave too subjective an interpretation to the things he observed on earth, which, incidentally, Faust repeatedly pointed out to him. (One need but recall their numerous heated arguments and debates.)

"Perhaps the beings who sent Mephistopheles to the Earth foresaw that the information he obtained would tend to be biased and subjective and, hence, erroneous. For this reason (and here I come to the focal point of my hypothesis,) Mephistopheles was instructed to take back to Em a terrestrial denizen, who would possess a much better understanding of his native planet's affairs than a visitor from another world. To be sure, as often as not we ourselves do not understand what goes on in our house, but the Emian scientists may not have been aware of this.

"Thus, Mephistopheles was to bring an Earthman with him back to Em. Naturally enough, he tried to get hold of a well-educated person. So after weighing the matter, he quite naturally chose—not a nobleman, nor even a king—but a serious scientist, one whose encyclopedic knowledge and scientific integrity were beyond the shadow of doubt. This, then, is why Mephistopheles needed Faust and no other man.

"Having reached this stage of our reasoning we may inquire whether the venerable scientist had any inkling of who Mephistopheles really was. The answer is no. Neither did Mephistopheles make any attempt to explain this to Faust. More—and this is a significant detail—I suspect Mephistopheles himself did his best to convince Faust that he had arrived straight from Hades. And this is why.

"Suppose the devil were to come to Earth today and call upon a contemporary scientist. How would he introduce himself? As the devil? By no means! For in that case he would have to spend a long time convincing the nonbelieving scholar that it wasn't a practical joke. But if a clever devil, taking account of the general interest in cosmic problems so characteristic of our time, were to introduce himself as a visitor from outer space, the scientist would be duly impressed and interested and agree to follow him anywhere.

"In the conditions of the Middle Ages, if Mephistopheles had ventured to tell Faust the truth, the latter would surely have assumed that his visitor was stark raving mad. Moreover, to convince the mediaeval scholar that he had actually come form another planet, Mephistopheles would have to explain things ranging from the fact that the Earth revolves around the sun to relativity theory, quantum physics, and the principle of operation of a photon motor. Undoubtedly Faust, in spite of his great education and erudition, would have been quite incapable of digesting all that information, and the result could be the opposite of that which Mephistopheles had set out to achieve. How much simpler it was to pose as a representative of the nether world, association with whom was considered wicked but nevertheless common enough. As we know, Faust readily accepted the explanation, especially as Mephistopheles exploited the other unknown achievements of science and technology to pass through walls, fly, become invisible—in short do all the things which served in Faust's eyes as irrefutable proof of Mephistopheles' demonic origin.

"But why, you may ask, did Mephistopheles waste so much time to gain Faust's confidence? Couldn't he simply have whisked Faust away to Em? Why did he need the old man's signature?

"I think the explanation is the mental attitude of the Emians. At a time when oppression and lawlessness dominated on Earth, on Em democracy was so highly developed and freedom of the individual was set so high that any coercion of an individual, even one from another planet, would have been absolutely impermissible. Mephistopheles was well aware that if he broke this code, he would be in for trouble, which is why he needed Faust's signature to confirm that the latter had left the Earth of his own free will. And as we know, he obtained the signature by convincing the scientist that he was merely signing a covenant whereby he delivered his soul into the hands of the devil.

"At this point a rather delicate point arises: How could a representative of a highly advanced civilization, brought up in a spirit of boundless respect for the individual, stoop to deceive an old man who had done him no harm? How *could* he have exploited Faust's ignorance to meet his own selfish purpose? This would certainly have been quite inexplicable if we overlooked the fact that Mephistopheles had been in contact with people for a long time. And the milieu, as we know, influences the mentality of every intelligent being.

"Finally, there is the question of Mephistopheles' external appearance. It could, of course, be suggested that the cosmic visitor decked himself out with horns, tail, hairy skin and other accessories to be in keeping with Faust's ideas of what the devil should look like. However, I think this was not the case. After all, the Emians need not resemble human beings in all details, and they could well have horns, tails, and so on. These could be rudimentary organs, like man's appendix, or they could be organs designed for specific functions. The horns, for example, could be a kind of U-shaped antennae for receiving telepathic messages. (We know that Mephistopheles could read thoughts.) Then the tail could be the ground connection. If we recall that sparks can be made to fly off a cat's fur, we can conjecture that the dense hairy growth of the Emians represents an accumulator and source of electricity for powering biological amplifiers of telepathic devices.

"But how is it, we may ask, that the Emians' external appearance so closely approximates common notions of what the devil is like? This, I should say, is a classical example of an interchange of cause and effect. Who, indeed, can claim that Mephistopheles was the first Emian to visit the earth?

Is it so implausible to conjecture that Emians had been sending expeditions to our planet from times immemorial? Then legends of meetings with the devil are simply reflections of encounters with the mysterious Emians, encounters which led to the development of the popular image of the devil.

"Why have such encounters ceased in the last few centuries? Perhaps the Emians are satisfied with their knowledge of us and have turned to other planets. Or, seeing that people are incapable of comprehending them, they have decided to wait till our civilization achieves the level necessary for mutual understanding and contact with intelligent beings from other planets.

"Perhaps this time has now come and we should be prepared that one fine day a visitor may call on any one of us and say, 'Good day, I am Mephistopheles.' "

With these words the young scientist looked at the audience for the last time, adjusted his fashionable tie, and, with a flourish of his hand, slowly melted from sight.

Translated by Vladimir Talmy.

Crabs Take Over the Island

ANATOLY DNIEPROV

1

"TAKE IT EASY, there!" Mr. Cookling—the engineer—shouted at the sailors who were standing up to their waists in the water and trying to get a small wooden box over the side of the launch. It was the last box of ten that the engineer had brought to the island.

"This heat's awful, a real inferno," moaned the engineer, wiping his thick red neck with a bandanna handkerchief. Then he peeled off his sweat-drenched shirt and threw it on the sand. "You can strip, Bud, there isn't any civilization here."

I looked dejectedly at the light schooner rolling gently on the waves a couple of miles off shore. She would be coming back for us in twenty days.

"Why the deuce did we have to come all this way to a solar hell with those machines of yours?" I asked Mr. Cookling as I pulled off my clothes. "With a sun like this we'll damn soon be roasting."

"Oh, don't worry about that, we'll be needing the sun pretty soon. Look, it's exactly noon now and the sun is right over head."

"It's always that way on the equator," I added in a mumble without taking my eyes off the *Turtle-Dove*—our schooner. "Any geography book'll tell you that."

The sailors came up and stood in front of the engineer, who slowly drew a roll of bills from his pocket.

"Will that be enough?" he asked extending a few.

One of them nodded.

"Then your job's done. You can return to the ship. Remind Captain Hale that we expect him back in exactly twenty days."

Mr. Cookling then turned to me. "Let's get started, Bud. I can't wait any more."

I looked at him long and hard.

"Frankly speaking, I don't know why we even came here. I realize of course that in the Admiralty you couldn't tell me anything. But now that we're here, I should think that you might."

Cookling made a wry face and looked intently at the sand.

"Well, yes, of course. Actually I could have told you before, but there just wasn't any time."

I felt that he was not telling the truth, but I didn't say anything. He continued to stand there rubbing his glistening red neck with a fat hand.

I knew the gesture. He invariable settled into this pattern when he wanted to lie his way out of a situation.

Yet even that suited me for the time being.

"You see, Bud, it's this way. We've got an amusing experiment under way here to test the theory of—what's his name—" here he paused and looked straight at me.

"Whose?"

"The Englishman. . . . Damn it all, the name just slipped —Oh yes, Darwin, Charles Darwin."

I went up to him and put my hand on his bare shoulder.

"Now listen, Mr. Cookling, don't take me for a moron. I know all about Darwin. Quit tacking about, just explain in a couple of words what brought us to this red-hot patch of sand in the middle of the ocean. And for pity's sake stop that Darwin stuff."

He laughed out loud, opening his mouth wide and exposing a full set of dentures. Then he took a few steps to one side and said, "You're impossible, Bud. That's exactly what we're going to test: Darwin's theory."

"You mean to tell me that's why we hauled ten boxes of hardware all this way?" I asked him, coming closer. I was seething with rage at this fat slob all glistening over with sweat.

"Exactly," he replied, and he wiped the smile from his face. "Now about your duties: you can start by opening Box No. 1. Take out the tent, water, canned food, and tools that we'll need to open the other boxes." Cookling spoke the same way that he had at the proving grounds when we were introduced. He was in military uniform then, and so was I.

"Very well," I said through clenched teeth and went up to Box No. 1.

A couple of hours later we had the tent up on the beach and we tossed into a corner a shovel, a crowbar, a hammer, a few screw-drivers, a chisel and various other tools. We also piled up about a hundred cans of food and tanks with fresh water.

Though Cookling was head of the operation, he worked like a horse. It was quite obvious he was eager to get things going. We were so busy in fact that we did not notice the *Turtle-Dove* weigh anchor and disappear from view.

After dinner we opened up Box No. 2. It contained an ordinary two-wheel cart of the kind used by porters at railway stations.

I started on the third box, but the engineer stopped me.

"Let's first get a look at the map. The rest of the cargo will have to be spread out over a variety of sites."

This stumped me.

"That's the way the experiment goes," he explained.

The island was round like an upturned plate, with a tiny bay towards the north, exactly where we unloaded. It was bounded by a sandy beach about fifty yards wide. Beyond was a slightly elevated plateau all covered over with stunted bushes that were bone-dry from the heat.

The island was no more than two miles across. There were several red marks on the map: some along the sandy beach, others in the interior.

"Everything we open up from now on will have to be carried out to these sites," Cookling explained.

"What are they, measuring instruments?"

"No," the engineer said with a chuckle. It was irritating, that chuckle of his. He would always turn it on when he knew something you didn't.

The third box was extremely heavy. I was positive it contained a machine, but when the first boards came loose I was dumbfounded. Out came sheets of steel and metal bars of different sizes and shapes. The whole box was packed with these metallic items.

"Looks like a kid's constructor set to me," I exclaimed tossing out heavy rectangles, cubes, and spheres—all metal.

"Hardly," the engineer replied and went for the next box.

Box No. 4 and the remaining ones up to number nine contained the same kinds of metal blanks. They were of three kinds: grey, red, and silverish. I could see right off that they were made of iron, copper, and zinc.

When I started to open the last box, No. 10, Cookling said: "We'll open that one after we deliver the other ones to their sites."

During the next three days, Cookling and I carted the pieces of metal to different parts of the island. We dumped them here and there in little piles. Some were left right on the ground. Others, on the engineer's instructions, I buried in the sand. Some piles were of similar iron bars, others contained a variety of types.

When we finished we returned to the tent for the tenth box.

"Open this one with particular care," Cookling ordered.

Box No. 10 was much lighter than the others and a bit smaller in size.

Inside we dug through compressed sawdust and at last

came to a package wrapped in flannel and wax paper. We unwrapped the package.

What appeared was the strangest-looking instrument I ever saw. At first glance it resembled a large metal toy in the shape of a crab. Yet this was no simple crab. In addition to six big segmented appendages, there were two pairs of slender tentacles that terminated in a half-open "maw" which jutted out of this monstrosity of a beast. On the back, slightly depressed, was a tiny parabolic mirror made of highly polished metal with a dark-red crystal in the center. Unlike toy crabs, this one had two pairs of eyes: in front and in back.

I stood for some time gaping at the creature.

"How do you like it?" Cookling asked at last.

I shrugged.

"It's a dangerous toy all right," said the engineer with obvious self-satisfaction. "You'll see for yourself. Pick it up and put it on the sand."

The crab was not heavy at all, weighing only about six or seven pounds. And it stood rather solidly on the sand.

"Well, what do we do now?" I asked the engineer with a touch of irony.

"Just wait a bit, let it warm up."

We both sat down on the sand and kept our eyes on the metal freak. In about two minutes I noticed the mirror on its back slowly begin to turn towards the sun.

"Look, it's coming to life," I exclaimed and jumped to my feet.

When I rose, my shadow accidentally fell on the machine and the crab suddenly went into motion, propelled by its paws; it made for the sunlight again. It was all so unexpected that I jumped aside.

"That's what kind of a toy it is," said Cookling, laughing. "Frightened a bit, huh?"

I touched my forehead, sweat was streaming down it.

"Come on, Cookling, what's all this about? Why did we come here after all?"

Cookling rose to his feet and came towards me; he was serious again.

"To test Darwin's theory."

"Yes, but Darwin's is a biological theory, the theory of natural selection of evolution and so on. . . . " I mumbled.

"Exactly! Look, our hero's decided he needs a drink of water!"

I was amazed. The toy crab was crawling towards the water. It lowered its proboscis and was obviously sucking up water. After quenching its thirst it crawled out into the sun again and came to a halt.

I kept watching the little machine and felt a strange revulsion mixed with fear. For a moment the clumsy toy crab seemed to resemble Cookling himself.

Then I asked the engineer: "Did you build it?"

"Ahuh," he muttered and stretched out on the sand.

I lay down too but did not take my eyes off of the strange device. Now it appeared to be quite lifeless.

Crawling on my belly I came up closer and examined the creature in more detail.

The back of the crab was in the form of a semi-cylindrical surface with flat ends front and back. There I found the two sets of holes that resembled eyes. The impression was heightened by the fact that deep down inside the body were brilliantly sparkling crystals. Underneath the crab was a flat platform—a belly of sorts. Somewhat above the level of the platform were three extended pairs of large-sized segmented nippers and two pairs of small ones.

I couldn't get a view of the insides of the crab.

Looking at this toy, I tried to figure out why the Admiralty attached so much importance to it and had chartered a special ship to this distant island for tests.

Cookling and I sat there on the sand until the sun had dropped so close to the horizon that the shadows from the bushes in the distance fell on our metal crab. It immediately responded by moving towards the sun. But the shade caught up with it again, and then it started to crawl along the shore, moving closer and closer to the water, which was still illuminated by the sun's rays. Sunlight seemed to be absolutely necessary for it.

We got up and slowly followed the little machine. In this way we gradually moved around the island until we were finally on the western side.

Here, almost on the shore, was the first of the piles of metal bars. When the crab had come within about ten yards of the pile, it suddenly seemed to forget all about the sun, made rapidly for the pile and came to a halt right near one of the copper bars.

Cookling touched my arm and said, "Let's go back to the tent. Things will develop tomorrow morning."

In the tent we had supper and then went to bed. I felt Cookling was pleased that I had not asked any more questions. Before falling asleep I noticed that he was restless, turned from side to side and occasionally chuckled. Which, of course, meant that he knew something that I was to learn about later.

2

Next morning I went for a swim in the warm water and watched the beautiful purple sky of dawn reflected in the rolling surface of the sea. I swam for a long time and when I got back to the tent the engineer was not there.

He's gone to take a look at his ugly mechanical mug, I mused, and opened a can of pineapples. I had hardly swallowed my third piece when I heard the voice of the engineer in the distance.

"Lieutenant, come here, look! It's begun, hurry up. Hurry up!"

I rushed out of the tent and saw Cookling up in the bushes on a hill waving his arms.

"Hurry up," he said. "Come on."

"Where?" I wondered.

"Right where we left our beauty yesterday."

The sun was already high in the sky when we reached

the first pile of metal bars sparkling in the bright rays. At first I couldn't make out anything.

It was only when I was a few steps from the pile that I noticed two fine jets of bluish smoke rising upwards and then. . . . I stopped stock-still. I rubbed my eyes. Was I seeing things? But no, the picture did not change. Near the pile of metal bars were two crabs, both exactly like the one that we had extracted from the box the day before.

"Did we actually miss one under the pile of bars?" I exclaimed.

Cookling squatted, chuckling and rubbing his hands.

"Quit this smartie business!" I cried. "Where'd the other crab come from?"

"It was born here last night, that's where it came from."

I bit my lip and without saying a word came closer to the crabs and noticed tiny wreaths of smoke rising from their backs. For a moment I was sure it was all a dream, hallucinations—both crabs were hard at work!

That's just it. They were really working. They were using their slender front tentacles to contact the bars and produce electric arcs that melted off chunks of metal. Then they pulled the pieces through their wide-open jaws. Something hummed inside these steel beings. From time to time a hissing sound came from their mouths, and a shaft of sparks followed, then a second pair of feelers extracted a finished part.

The separate elements were then assembled on the flat under-platform in a specific sequence and gradually emerged as a whole from under the crab.

On the platform of the first crab was a third crab almost completely assembled. The second crab was still working on the outlines of his mechanism. I was struck dumb.

"Why these creatures are multiplying," I screamed.

"Exactly. The sole purpose of this machine is to manufacture duplicates of itself. It's a replicating device," explained Cookling.

"But how is it possible?" I yelled, unable to grasp anything any more.

"Why not? Take any simple machine tool. It produces parts of itself, single elements. That's where I got the idea of an automated machine that would be able to turn out all its parts from start to finish. The crab is an analogue of just such a machine."

I stood there trying to comprehend what the engineer had said. At the same time I noticed that the first crab had opened its mouth and was spitting out a broad sheet of metal. It covered the assembled mechanism on the platform, thus creating the back for the third automation. When the back was mounted properly, the forward paws deftly welded into place, in front and back, metallic walls with apertures—and a new crab was born. Like its brothers, on its back it had a bright sparkling metal mirror, somewhat depressed, with a red crystal in the center.

The crab "mother" pulled up the platform under its belly and the "baby" plumped down onto the sand, its paws outspread. I noticed that the mirror on its back slowly sought out the sun. After standing for some time the crab sauntered off towards the beach for a drink of water. Then it climbed back and stood motionless, basking in the sunlight.

I was surely dreaming, I thought.

While I was examining the newly born crab, Cookling said, "Look, there's a fourth crab ready."

I turned and saw a fourth crab that had just been born.

Meanwhile the first two stood near the pile of metal as if nothing concerned them, yet they continued to snip off pieces of metal and gulp them down, repeating all the operations that we had just viewed.

The fourth crab likewise moved off for a drink of sea water.

"What do they have to drink water for?" I asked.

"That's the way they fill up their storage batteries. In the sunlight, the solar energy is converted into electricity by means of a silicon battery and the mirror on the crab's back.

It is sufficient to recharge the storage battery and for handling day-time operations. At night the robot is powered by the energy stored up during the sunny day.

"So they can work day and night?"

"That's right, day and night, without let-up."

The third crab began to move towards the pile of metal bars.

Now there were three automatic creatures at work; the fourth was charging up with solar power.

"But there isn't any material for silicon batteries in these piles of metal," I ventured, trying to get at the technology of this self-replication of machines.

"That's something we don't need to worry about." And the engineer kicked the sand with his boot. "Sand is nothing but silica. Using the electric arc process, the crab is able to produce pure silicon."

We returned to the tent in the evening, and by that time there were six robots hard at work on the pile of metal, and two more were basking in the warm rays of the sun.

"What are these creatures for?" I asked Cookling at supper.

"For war. These crabs represent a terrifying tool of sabotage," he said quite frankly.

"I don't get you," I said.

"Do you know what a progression is?"

"Well, yes, so what?"

"Yesterday we began with a single crab. Right now there are eight out there. Tomorrow there will be sixty-four, the day after tomorrow there will be five hundred and twenty, and so on. In ten days we will have ten million crabs, for which we will have to have thirty thousand tons of metal."

I staggered under the onslaught of numbers.

"But still. . . ."

"These crabs will be able, in short order, to gobble up all the metal the opposing side possesses: tanks, aircraft, everything. Every machine, all mechanisms, devices and pieces of metal. All the metal in the country. A month later there will not be a single piece of metal in the whole world. Everything will be used up to reproduce crabs. And, as you know, metal is all-important in time of war; it's a strategic material of the highest priority."

"So that is why the Admiralty became so excited over your toy!" I whispered.

"Precisely. But this is only the first model. I plan to simplify it drastically and in that way speed up the process of reproducing the robots. We could accelerate it, say, by two or three times. The design could be made more stable and rigid. They could also be made more mobile. We could likewise refine the sensitivity of the indicators for searching out deposits of metal. Then in time of war my automatons will be more terrible than plague. I want to be able to wipe out the entire metal potential of the enemy in a matter of two or three days.

"Yes, but when the metal-eaters have cleaned up the territory of the enemy they will crawl over to our side and do the same!" I exclaimed.

"That is question number two. The operations of these robots can be coded so that if we know the code the process they can be stopped as soon as they appear on our side. Incidentally, that is one way of bringing all the metal reserves of the enemy onto our side."

That night I had horrible nightmares. Swarms of steel crabs were climbing over me, swishing their feelers, and emitting tiny swirls of blue smoke from their metallic bodies.

3

Engineer Cookling's automatic crabs practically covered the whole island in four days.

According to his calculations, there were now over four thousand of them.

Their glinting bodies could be seen everywhere. When the metal in one pile gave out, they searched the island for new piles and found them.

On the fifth day, just before the sun went down, I witnessed a terrible scene. Two crabs were fighting over a piece of zinc.

This was on the southern tip of the island where we had buried a number of zinc bars in the sand. The crabs working at different sites would periodically come here to manufacture a required zinc part. This time it happened that there were some twenty crabs there at the pit at the same time trying to get the zinc they needed, and a real battle ensued. The mechanical beings got in each other's way. There was one crab that seemed to me more adroit, perhaps simply more arrogant and stronger.

Pushing aside his fellow robots, he proceeded to climb onto their backs in frenzied attempts to extract a piece of metal from the bottom of the pit. When he was almost within reach of one, another crab grasped the piece with its claws. Then a tug of war resulted. The one that I had picked as being nimbler finally pulled the bar away from its opponent. But this one in turn did not want to give up the booty and, manoeuvering from behind, it lay down on top of the other robot and thrust its slender tentacles into its mouth.

The feelers of the first and second crabs were locked in a struggle and with terrifying might they proceeded to pull each other to pieces.

None of the other machines paid the slightest attention, though this was quite obviously a life and death struggle. Suddenly the crab that had been on top fell back belly upwards and the iron platform slid down revealing its mechanical innards. At that very instant, its opponent flashed out with an electric arc and began to slice up his adversary. When the body fell to pieces, the victor extracted levers, gears, wires, and tossed them into its mouth, as fast as it could.

As the new parts entered the voracious mechanical beast, the platform moved out and I could see a new mechanical crab being assembled frantically.

Another few minutes, and a freshly born metal crab flopped off the platform onto the sand.

When I told Cookling what I had witnessed, he only chuckled.

"That's exactly what I need," he said.

"But why?"

"Well, didn't I tell you that I want to perfect my mechanical creatures?"

"True, but all you need to do is take your drawings and conjure up something more exotic. Why the need for this fighting? Pretty soon they'll start devouring each other!"

"That's just what is required! The survival of the fittest!"

I thought a bit and then objected.

"What do you mean by fittest? They're all the same. As far as I can see, they simply multiply, reproducing copies of themselves."

"What do you think, is it possible—speaking generally—to manufacture identical copies? Even ball bearings never come out the same in every respect. Here the matter is infinitely more involved. The manufacturing automaton has a guiding device that compares the copy with the original design. Can you imagine what would happen if every new item came out different from the original but like its immediate predecessor? Before long we would have a mechanism totally different from the progenitor."

"But if it is not like the original, it will not fulfill its basic function—that of reproducing itself," I objected.

"So what? All the better in fact. Another robot will generate better items out of the corpse. The more refined replicates will be those that quite accidentally accumulate peculiarities of design that will make them more viable. In that way, we will have generations of stronger, faster and simpler creatures. That is why I do not intend to sit down to any drawings. All I need to do is wait until my mechanical beings eat up all the metal on the island and begin a war in which they will devour one another and reproduce new versions again and again. That is how I will get the ultimate devices I need."

That night I did not sleep a wink. I simply sat on the

sandy beach in front of the tent and smoked cigarette after cigarette. Could it really be that Cookling had thought up an operation that would threaten mankind at large? Were we, on this godforsaken island, breeding a terrible plague capable of removing all the metal from the earth?

While I was thus meditating, a number of metal creatures rushed past me, clanking and squeaking, tirelessly at work within themselves. One of the crabs ran into me and I gave it a terrific kick. Helplessly, if flipped over on its back belly upwards. In a split second two other crabs were on it flashing their electric arcs in the darkness.

The miserable creature was slashed to shreds! That was enough for me. Too much in fact. I hurried to the tent and took a crowbar from one of the boxes. Cookling was snoring peacefully.

Approaching the swarm of crabs stealthily, I swung at one of them with all my might.

For some reason, my idea was that this would frighten the rest. But nothing happened. The other crabs plunged for the victim and sparks flared once again.

I struck some more blows, but this only increased the number of sparks. More mechanical beasts were arriving from deep inside the island.

In the darkness I saw only the outlines of these devices and in the melee one of them appeared to be much bigger than the others.

That was the one I went for. But when I connected with the crow-bar I got a terrible electric shock. Somehow the metal beast had acquired an electric potential. The first thing that came to mind was that evolution had produced a defence reaction.

Shaking all over, I approached the buzzing swarm of robots to retrieve my weapon. But that was too much to hope for. What I saw in the dark was my crow-bar being sliced to pieces in the flickering light of electric arcs. The big robot that I had wanted to knock out was by far the better one at this job.

There was nothing for me to do but return to the tent and go to bed. For a time I escaped reality in deep slumber. But it was soon over. I awakened suddenly and was conscious of something cold and heavy moving over my body. I jumped to my feet. Before I could grasp what had taken place, the crab had vanished into a corner of the tent. Seconds later I saw a brilliant scintillation—the typical electric spark. The abominable device was in search of metal and had thrust its electrode towards one of the cans containing fresh water and was cutting it to pieces!

I gave Cookling a push to wake him up and tried to explain the matter in a few words.

"Get all the cans into the water, into the sea. All food into the sea!" he ordered.

We started dragging our cans to the sea and laid them on the sandy bottom at waist depth. We did the same with our tools.

After that strenuous operation we sat on the beach till morning sleepless, wet all over and totally exhausted. Cookling breathed heavily and I was actually pleased that he was suffering from his crazy idea. But now I was full of hatred and maliciously desired a graver punishment for him.

4

I don't remember how much time passed since we arrived on the island, but one fine day Cookling stated triumphantly. "The most exciting thing is about to take place. All the metal has been devoured."

True enough, all the caches of bars, slabs and other pieces of metal were gone. Empty pits could be seen here and there along the shore.

All metal cubes, bars and rods had been turned into mechanical robots that were now swarming over the island. Their movements were swift and jerky; the storage batteries were charged to the limit, and no energy was being expended in actual work. These mechanical creatures wandered down the shore line, crawled in among the bushes on the plateau, colliding with each other and frequently with us too.

Watching them, I realized that Cookling was right. The crabs were actually different. They differed in overall dimensions, the size of the claws and the volume of the workshop maws. Some were more mobile than the others; apparently there were differences in their internal workings as well.

"Well," Cookling mused, "it's about time they began to quarrel."

"Do you really mean it?" I asked.

"Most definitely. Cobalt is the catalyst in this case. The mechanism is devised in such fashion that intake of the tiniest quantity of cobalt will, so to speak, suppress their mutual respect for each other."

The next morning, Cookling and I set off for our "marine storehouse." From the bottom of the sea, just off shore, we extracted a number of cans, some water and four heavy grey bars of cobalt which the engineer had kept reserved specially for the decisive stage of his experiment.

When Cookling came out onto the sand carrying the cobalt bars high over his head, several crabs thrust themselves towards him. They did not go beyond the shadow of his body, but you could readily see that the new metal had upset them very much. I stood a number of paces away from the engineer and was surprised to see two robots make awkward jumps.

"Just look at that variety of movements! Notice how different they all are. The fratricidal war that we are about to initiate will eliminate all but the strongest and fittest. And they in turn will generate still better offspring." Then he heaved the cobalt bars into the bushes one after the other.

What followed is hard to describe.

Several robots made a mad rush for the bars; pushing and jostling one another they set about cutting the bars with their electric sparks. Others impatiently crowded up from behind striving to get at a piece of metal when the opportunity came. Some climbed over the backs of their comrades in attempts to get to the center.

"There it is: the first real fight!" shouted the engineer with glee and clapped his hands.

Within minutes the site had turned into a fierce battleground with more and more crabs crashing into the melee.

As parts of cut-up devices and cobalt got into the mouths of fresh machines, they became wild, fearless robot predators and straightaway attacked their fellow creatures.

During the first stage of this war, the attackers were those that had partaken of cobalt. They were the ones that slashed to pieces the robots that were rushing in from all over the island in the hope of obtaining a bit of metal. But as more and more crabs got the taste of cobalt, the battle raged fiercer still. By this time, the new-born robots that had come to life in the midst of warfare were already entering the fray.

These were a remarkable generation of mechanical crabs! They were smaller in size and capable of amazing speeds. What struck me was the fact that they no longer felt the need of the traditional procedure of charging their batteries.

They found the solar energy that their much larger mirrors were absorbing to be quite sufficient. With an amazing ferocity they swung out at several crabs and slashed them to shreds, taking two or three at a time.

Cookling stood in the water beaming with boundless self-satisfaction. He rubbed his hands and grunted with delight.

"Oh, this is tremendous! Just wait and see what happens next!"

For me the conflict of clanging metal was abominable and fearful in the extreme. What monster would emerge from the struggle was uppermost in my mind.

By noon, the entire beach around our tent was one grand battlefield. Robots from all over the island had converged on this spot. The war went on without any shouts or cries or booming of guns or swishing of shells. In the new warfare, one heard the crackling of numerous electric sparks, the banging of metal against metal and a grinding and crunching and ringing of machine against machine.

Though for the most part the offspring was low-slung and extremely mobile, a new kind of device was emerging. The fresh species was larger than ever before. They were ponderous in their movements but possessed enormous strength and definitely had an edge over the tiny devices that were heedlessly throwing themselves into the assault.

When the sun began to set, there was a sudden change in the movements of the smaller machines: they crowded to the western side and slowed down.

"Oh, my God," exclaimed Cookling, "they are all doomed! These creatures are without storage batteries and life in them will cease as soon as the sun sets."

Which is what happened. As soon as the sun dropped low, and the bushes cast long shadows that covered the vast swarm of small-size robots, life ceased altogether. Instead of a host of ferocious aggressive beasts, the place was an enormous graveyard of lifeless metal.

Then the big three-feet-high crabs lumbered forth and ponderously took to devouring the little crabs one by one. On the platforms of the giant progenitors, offspring of fantastic proportions was in the making.

Cookling's face darkened. This kind of evolution was not in his calculations. Unwieldy mechanical crabs of such dimensions would definitely be a poor weapon for sabotage in the enemy rear.

It became rather peaceful on the beach as the giant crabs continued mopping up the small-size generation.

I stepped out of the water and the engineer followed. We walked along the eastern fringe of the island trying to collect our thoughts.

I was extremely tired and fell asleep almost as soon as I had stretched out on the warm soft sand.

5

I was jerked awake in the middle of the night by a terrifying scream. Getting to my feet, I saw only a greyish strip of sandy beach and the sea that merged with the black starry sky.

The cry came again, this time from the bushes, and then it was quiet. Only then did I notice that Cookling was no longer with me. I rushed in the direction of what seemed to be his voice.

The sea was calm, as usual, and the wavelets lapping the sand were fairly audible. But it seemed to me that the surface of the water was rather perturbed right over the cache containing our food and drinking-water tanks. Something was splashing and bubbling.

I figured it must be Cookling.

"Cookling, where are you?" I shouted approaching our underwater storehouse.

"I'm here!" said a voice off to the right.

"Where? I don't see you."

"Right here," came the engineer's voice. "I'm up to my neck in the water. Come over here."

I stepped into the water and stumbled over something hard. It was a huge crab standing in the deep water on high extended claws.

"Why did you get in so deep? What are you doing here?" I asked.

"They've been chasing me and they've cornered me!" he moaned.

"What do you mean, chasing? Who's been chasing you?"

"The crabs!"

"But why? They never go after me."

I stumbled again over one of the robots and then circled round it, finally reaching the engineer. Yes, he was indeed up to his neck in the water.

"Listen, what's all this about?"

"I don't know myself," he exclaimed in a shaky voice. "One of the robots attacked me while I was asleep. I thought it was just by accident, and so I moved to the side, but it kept closing in on me and touched my face with its claw. So I got up and jumped away. It went after me, and I started running. Then I noticed another one join in the chase. Then some more followed, a whole swarm. That's how they got me cornered here."

"But it's never happened before. And if their evolution had developed a man-hating instinct, they would not have spared me."

"I don't know what to think," whispered Cookling hoarsely. "But I'm afraid to come out onto the beach now."

"Why that's nonsense," I said, taking him by the hand. "Let's go along the shore towards the east, I'll watch out for you."

"How?"

"We'll go to the storehouse and I'll take some heavy object, say a hammer."

"No, for heaven's sake, nothing made of metal," groaned the engineer. "Better take a board from one of the boxes— something wooden."

We groped slowly along the shore line and when we reached the tool cache I left Cookling and approached the beach.

Loud splashes of water and the familiar humming of machinery could be heard.

The mechanical beasts were emptying our canned food. They had ferreted out our underwater storehouse.

"Cookling, we're lost!" I screamed. "They've eaten up all our cans."

"Oh, Lord, what are we going to do now?" he wailed.

"You better do some hard thinking, this was all your crazy idea. You've bred the weapon you dreamed of. Now get us out of this fix."

I skirted the mass of robots and came out onto the land.

Here, in the dark, I crawled among the crabs and collected a few pieces of meat scattered about on the sand, the remnants of canned pineapples, oranges and some other bits of food and carried everything to the sandy plateau above. Judging from the quantities of food strewn about the beach,

I could see that these beasts had been hard at work while we slept. I couldn't find a single can intact.

While I was busy gathering the remains of our food, Cookling stood in the water up to his neck some twenty paces from the shore.

I was so taken up with getting together at least a few scraps to eat and was so upset about what had occurred that I completely forgot about the existence of the engineer. However, he soon reminded me with a blood-curdling scream. And then: "Bud, for God's sake, help me, they're on me!"

I jumped into the water and rushed towards Cookling stumbling over our mechanical monsters. Here, about five steps from him, I tripped over one of the robots and stretched out full length.

The crab did not pay any attention to me.

"I'll be damned, what have they got against you? You're practically their father, you might say," I yelled.

"I don't know," whispered Cookling hoarsely, and the water gurgled round his head. "Do something, Bud, get him off me. If another crab is born any taller than this one, I'm a goner, for sure."

"That's evolution for you. Listen, what's the weakest spot in these contraptions? How should I strike for a knock-out?"

"Before the best way was to break the parabolic mirror or pull out the inner storage battery. Now, I really don't know. . . . Actually a special investigation is needed."

"To hell with your investigations," I yelled and grabbed one of the slender front paws of the crab that was almost touching the engineer's face.

The mechanical beast reared on its haunches. I searched out the second paw and tweaked it. The tentacles bent readily, like copper wire.

It was obvious that the robot did not like this operation at all and it slowly emerged from the water. The engineer and I then hastened along the shore.

When the sun rose, all the robots climbed out of the

water and stood motionless for some time warming up in the sun's rays. During this time I took a stone and broke most of the parabolic mirrors on the backs of a good fifty or so of the monsters. All motion ceased.

Unfortunately, this did not improve the situation any because they soon became the victims of other beasts, and these with amazing rapidity began generating fresh batches of robots. I simply did not have strength enough to break up the silicon batteries on the backs of all the machines. From time to time I came upon electrified robots and this weakened my resolve to wage any further warfare.

All this time, Cookling was standing offshore in the water.

The battle between our metallic monsters soon got under way again; they seemed to have forgotten the engineer completely.

We got away from the battle ground and headed to the other side of the island. The engineer was shivering so much from his many-hour vigil in the sea that he dropped to the ground, teeth chattering, and asked me to cover him up with hot sand.

After that I returned to our original camping site to get some clothing and anything in the way of food that I could pick up. It was only then I noticed that the tent was torn to pieces: the iron pegs that held down the ends of the tent were gone, the iron rings that held the ropes were nowhere to be found either.

Under the tarpaulin I found Cookling's clothes and my own. The crabs hadn't missed this opportunity either. All metal hooks, buttons and clasps were missing, and the cloth had been singed where each one had been torn out.

Meanwhile the battle-royal of robot devices had shifted inland away from the shore. When I reached the flat upper shelf of land I noticed a number of tall-legged creatures the height of a man moving in among the bushes near the center of the island. They were engaged in pairs, slowly moving away from each other and then rushing together at awful speeds. There was a terrible ringing and clanging of metal in each collision of these mechanical monsters. The ponderous movements of the giants with their enormous strength and great weight were petrifying.

Several robots were cut to the ground before my very eyes, and then devoured almost instantaneously.

But by this time I was fed up with all this fighting of machines run amok. I gathered up what I could of the things at our old site and went back to Cookling.

The sun was blistering hot and I had to take a dip or two before I reached the spot where I had dug the engineer into the sand.

I was approaching the sand mound where Cookling was sleeping after his night-long bathing sessions when I noticed a tremendous crab emerging from the bushes at the edge of the plateau.

It was taller than I and its paws were long and heavy. It moved with irregular jerks, bending its body in a strange fashion. The forward working tentacles were enormous and dragged along in the sand. But a real study in hypertrophic growth was the workshop maw of the monster. It was about half of the whole body.

Prehistoric, I mused. It crawled cumbersomely along the shore slowly turning its body from side to side, as if taking in the new scene. I involuntarily shook the tent canvas as one would have done to frighten a cow standing in one's path. But it paid no attention at all and continued to approach Cookling's mound of sand in a strange sidelike manner, describing a broad arc as it came in.

If I had only guessed that the monster was heading for the engineer, I would have rushed to his aid. But the trajectory of the robot was so indefinite that I was sure it was moving in the direction of the water. Only when it touched the water with its forward paws and then sharply turned and rushed towards the engineer did I drop my baggage and run as fast as I could.

The prehistoric mammoth of a machine stopped over Cookling and fell back on its haunches.

I noticed the ends of the feelers shiver in the sand right near the engineer's face.

The next instant, a cloud of sand shot up out of the mound. It was Cookling. Stung by the mechanical beast, he jumped up and tried to get away.

But it was already too late.

The thin tentacles had already wrapped themselves round his meat neck and were pulling him up into the maw of the robot. Cookling hung in the air helpless, throwing his arms and legs in every direction.

Though I hated the engineer with extreme bitterness, I could not allow him to perish in a struggle with such a brainless creature of metal.

Hardly giving myself time to reason, I grabbed the high claws of the crab and pulled with all the strength I had. But it was like trying to upturn a steel rod driven deep into the ground. The monster did not budge.

Then I drew myself up onto its back. For in instant, my face was level with Cookling's distorted features. His teeth, I realized suddenly, Cookling had steel teeth!

I hit the parabolic mirror with my fist as hard as I could. The crab began to jerk, Cookling's pallid face and bulging eyes were now at the entrance to the construction maw. What happened was terrible indeed. An electric spark jumped to his forehead and crossed his temple. Then the crab's tentacles suddenly relaxed and the senseless heavy body of the creator of this iron plague crumpled to the sand.

I stood in a daze, Cookling was stretched out on the sand dead. Round about us were several enormous mechanical crabs chasing each other. They did not pay the slightest attention to me or to the dead military engineer at my feet.

I wrapped Mr. Cookling up in the canvas of the tent and put him in a shallow sandy pit in the middle of the island. I buried him without any compunction. The sand crunched in my parched mouth and I cursed the engineer for his horrible invention.

Days passed by as I lay motionless on the shore peering into the distance from time to time, waiting for the return of the *Turtle-Dove*. Time dragged on interminably, the blistering sun seemed to hang over my head motionless. From time to time I crawled to the water and lowered my splitting head into it.

I tried to think in the abstract so as to curb my hunger and torturing thirst. For a moment my thoughts focused on brilliant minds that are nowadays spending all their time devising misery for others. Engineer Cookling's invention was such a case. I had been sure that we would be able to do great things with it. I figured we could have directed the evolution of these mechanical beings so that they might speed the solution of many problems. I even concluded that with appropriate refinements in the inner workings it would not have degenerated into an unwieldy monster of fantastic size.

Once, a huge shadow moved over me. I raised my head with great difficulty and saw that I was lying between the claws of a robot crab of tremendous proportions. It had come down to the beach and appeared to be scanning the coast line in wait of something.

I must have lost consciousness. In my heated brain the giant crab turned into a tall tank of fresh water that was just beyond my reach.

I regained consciousness only on board the schooner. When Captain Hale asked me whether they should also take along the enormous machine lying on the beach, I said I didn't think there was any need to.

Translated by GEORGE YANKOVSKY.

The Garden

GENNADY GOR

1

"SID, do you think that sociologist understands?"

"He seems to, Nina; one of his questions was quite unusual."

"What do you mean, unusual? Are you saying that he actually asked how you happen to be here, in this century?"

"Yes."

"Did you tell him?"

"Of course."

"But did he believe you?"

"Who knows? I wrote the word 'FUTURE' in capital letters. At first he thought I was born in a settlement named 'Future' somewhere on the edge of Antarctica. I think I set him straight, though."

"But don't you see; you can't explain something like that! Sociologists recognize only cold, hard fact."

"Some fact! A man born in the twenty-first century suddenly materializes in the twentieth. Didn't he demand any proofs from you?"

"Not yet. He'll be back for them. He was searching for the norm, the typical, statistically verifiable rule of behavior. Instead, when he ran up against something so out of the ordinary, I thought he'd have a stroke. He looked at me as if I were crazy, and then ripped his questionnaire into shreds. When he quieted down and we began to talk, he asked me if I had answered him in a metaphysical sense.

'No,' I answered, 'I really was born in the twenty-first century, and that is no metaphor.' He replied that my answer did come under the heading of philosophy, and was indeed a metaphor. He surprised me, though—in the end he believed me."

"He believed you? No—I think he merely pretended to. It's not likely that a social scientist would believe in an event which contradicts logic."

"But, Nina, he seemed to believe it. That is, at first he didn't—but then he began to be convinced. I answered all his questions about the twenty-first century. But enough about the sociologist, Nina. We can talk more about him after I finish my work."

Sid was doing a sketch of a tree on a large sheet of paper, while Nina rocked away in her rocking-chair reading poetry from a slim, elegant book. From time to time she looked at the picture of the poet on the book jacket. The poet looked like Sid. Indeed, the resemblance was so striking that Nina became more and more agitated with each glance at the cover. Of course, the poet could not be Sid, nor Sid the poet. After all, they were born two centuries apart.

"Sidney—last night I woke up and you were gone. Where were you?"

"Behind the window."

"What were you doing there?"

"I wasn't *doing* anything, just standing there."

"Why?"

"How many times have I told you that at night I transform myself into a garden? They taught me that there."

"Where?"

"In the future."

"In the town Future?" said Nina in a mocking illusion to the sociologist.

"No—in the Future which will be."

"Only in a fairy tale can a man turn into a garden. But you're not living in a fairy tale. I hope you didn't tell the sociologist that you turn yourself into a garden at night!"

"I did tell him."

"Why?"

"He wanted to know what I feel when I am drawing my pictures. He wanted to know absolutely everything that I experience inwardly, what I think about. He wanted to enter into my soul and I let him in. . . . "

Nina laughed bitterly. "You let in a sociologist but not your wife. We've been together a year and I know nothing about your past."

"My past is the future. My life starts not at the beginning, but at the end. I have never concealed that. The date in my passport confuses everyone."

"A mistake of the passport office," Nina maintained stubbornly.

"No, only a tiny inaccuracy. They wrote the year 2003, but the twenty-first century is still twenty-five years away. I hurried, Nina, and came to the earth ahead of time instead of waiting for the date which fate had assigned to me. In my world the element of chance has been banished; people are no longer born accidentally."

2

Nina met Sid in a garden. She sat on a bench and, laying her book aside, listened intently to the noise of the branches. The wind blew; the garden rustled around her. Suddenly, without warning, a silence fell. It was strange and inexplicable, even eerie. The wind was blowing as before but the branches neither swayed nor made a sound. The garden had become as silent as the reflection in a pond.

Nina heard footsteps. A young man appeared in front of her, holding a branch bursting with cherry blossoms.

"You are not allowed to break off branches here," said Nina severely. "Who are you?"

"Who am I *now?*" asked the young man, "or who I was five minutes ago?"

"Have you managed to change completely in five minutes?"

"Yes, I did! I hurried because I wanted to make your acquaintance. I've often seen you here with your book."

"You must be mistaken, I've never seen you."

"Of course you've seen me, but you didn't know that it was I. I didn't look quite as I do now."

"What did you look like?"

"You wouldn't believe me if I told you."

"Why not? You have such an honest face. You don't look like a fraud. How did you look?"

"Later!" said the young man nervously. "It's not important how I looked half an hour ago. What is important is how I look now."

"Now you look like a man who has just passed an important test."

"A good guess!" In fact, I have just passed a test. I have become a man all over again."

"And just what were you before?"

"I was a garden," he answered quietly.

"A what?"

"A garden."

"A garden; I don't quite understand. A garden can't turn into a man."

"It can. But then, I have not always been a garden—only occasionally when I really wanted to be one."

"Did some evil magician turn you into a garden?"

"No, not an evil one. A rather kind one in fact. But that's a secret, and I'm not allowed to talk about it. I promised."

"Promised whom?"

"The director of the *ISFT,* the Institute of Sorcerers and Fairy Tales."

"And where is this institute?"

"Well, it doesn't exist as yet. But it will! I, too, am not supposed to exist, but I rushed things and here I am. I couldn't allow fate to keep us apart. I've come from a century that is yet to be. In order to see you every day, I turned into a garden. I stood here in the rain, through storms and hot spells, just waiting for you."

"You must be some kind of a crank or eccentric. You keep bringing up impossible things."

"For you it's impossible, but for me it's possible. In the ISFT they had learned to transform people into natural phenomena. But this ancient art has been forgotten. Don't you see, I am an artist. Becoming a garden helps me in my work. I rarely paint portraits. I do landscapes. Soon an exhibition of my paintings will be held at the Russian Museum. I'll send you a ticket for the opening."

3

It was a formal invitation, printed in red and black:

THE LENINGRAD BRANCH OF THE UNION OF ARTISTS OF RSFSR AND THE RUSSIAN GOVERNMENT MUSEUM INVITE YOU TO THE OPENING OF AN EXHIBIT OF WORKS BY SIDNEY NIKOLAEVICH OBLAKOV.

"So, it turns out he really has a name, a patronymic and a surname. His last name is Oblakov . . . Cloud . . . How well it fits him!"

Nina studied the ticket and the catalogue with curiosity: Paintings, drawings, water colors, graphics, prints. Amazing! It turned out that he also illustrated children's books. At the publishing house, no one can have known that he was able to turn into a garden.

. . . Nina went to the museum. It was crowded. A grey-haired venerable, art critic opened the exhibition. He spoke clearly and solemnly:

"Sidney Nikolaevich Oblakov, inspite of his youth, has already succeeded in saying something new in art. His water colors are full of enchantment as if the paper had actually absorbed the blue of the sky, the lustre of a cloud, the freshness of the morning dew."

Oblakov stood near the critic. At that moment one could almost believe that he had come out of another age.

Nina smiled at him, but he didn't notice because of the crowd. A good-looking girl, one of the museum's employees, handed the old critic a pair of scissors and he awkwardly cut the ribbon. Nina flowed into the exhibit hall along with the rest of the crowd.

Pausing near the first water color, Nina saw herself through the artist's eyes. He had used pure water colors and her face shone as if through the water of a country stream. Clean, cold, fresh water had washed over her image, sweeping away all that was commonplace and incidental. In the water color she had become an integral part of nature, of the woods, of the pond, of the clouds which were reflected in the stream.

Suddenly she heard a clear voice:

"How happy I am that you came!"

Sid was standing beside her.

"Are you Oblakov?" asked Nina. "I didn't know you had a full name."

He smiled: "Well, yes I do. A garden can't have a name; a garden is just part of nature. But people aren't accepted into the Union of Artists unless they have a full name. I was forced to go to the police to get a passport. Besides, being a garden is only my avocation. Those are my two professions —being an artist and being a garden."

"Why do you masquerade as a garden? It's absurd."

"I don't claim to be a garden: the garden claims to be me. While I was waiting for you I was a garden, but when you arrived I turned into a man."

"You speak so strangely. Once upon a time, when I was a child, a fairy tale used to speak to me that way."

"Your childhood has returned. Again you find yourself in a fairy tale world—a world where there are no barriers between things, events, and human beings. But more about that later. Now I want you to look over my landscapes."

Pushing his way through the crowd, he led her up to his

landscapes. Everyone recognized him. Behind her she over-heard two artists:

"He studied in Paris with Matisse himself."

"How could he have studied with Matisse? Matisse died ages ago!"

"Look at the catalog. In the introductory article it says he is a student of Matisse!"

Nina asked Oblakov: "Did you study with Matisse?"

"Yes," he answered quietly.

"But you know that Matisse died before you were born!"

"Before . . . after . . . it's inconsequential. I was born in the future and have appeared here in your century. I visited Matisse. I turned into a garden under his window. He drew me and we became friends."

"Why do you speak so strangely?"

"I'm telling you the truth. It's difficult to recognize it in the light of day-to-day logic, but easy to do so in the logic of the fairy-tale world. There is a fairy-tale relationship between us. But let's not go into that now. Now I want you to look at that landscape over there. It's called 'Garden.' Do you recognize it?"

She knew it at once. It was the very same garden where they had met. But it was also a garden and a man simultaneously as in Ovid's Metamorphoses. The youth depicted in it was at one with nature. It was as though he had not yet become separate and distinct from Nature. The colors were like the morning, and fresh as a ripple on the blue surface of a pond. The painting seemed like music transformed somehow into clean, pure flowers squeezed out of a tube onto the paper; or rather, not from a tube, but straight from a living branch, from real grass, from the dawn itself. On paper the artist had caught the vivid, tender tones of that garden, as if it was right there in front of them together with the wind and the morning.

"Matisse especially liked this water color," he said quietly.

"Matisse died about fifty years ago."

"I was there then."

"How could you have been. You don't look over twenty-five years old!"

"That's not important. I can be both younger and older than myself. Here comes an art critic. He's pushing his way toward us. Judging from his expression I don't expect anything good."

Nina stepped aside. From time to time she looked at the paunchy face of the critic which was getting gloomier every minute.

Nina stopped at the water color on the wall before her. It was a wide window thrown open onto spring in the forest. There seemed to be an oriole near a window pouring forth his liquid, flowing whistle.

Sidney had succeeded with his colors alone in transmitting something inncommunicable: a bird's whistle. Then a cuckoo began to 'sing.' The forest absorbed the sound and sent it back to her.

Nina listened closely. Now she heard a voice, no longer that of the cuckoo—it was the critic saying angrily:

"Just sketches—sketches are not a picture. Just colors, and colors are not a subject. You've had little training. Matisse taught you nothing."

4

In the Marriage Bureau they asked Sid:

"Mr. Oblakov, when were you born?"

"2003."

The registrar smiled: "B.C.?"

"No, A.D."

"But it's only 1975 now."

"If you don't believe me, look at my passport."

The young man opened the passport and his face darkened.

"I'll register you, Comrade Oblakov, but you must correct the obvious error in this document. You couldn't have been born in a century that is still in the future."

"Yes, I could."

"Let's not get into an argument. After all, this is just the Marriage Bureau."

What would have happened to this polite young man if he had known that Sid Oblakov really was twenty years younger than himself. But neither Sid nor Nina bothered to try and explain. They got their mariage certificate and hailed a cab for home.

The taxi driver eavesdropped nervously on their conversation. Within five minutes he had become extremely upset and twice nearly wrecked the cab. He recognized familiar words but couldn't make heads or tails out of their conversation. This driver liked order—a place for everything and everything in its place; words, deeds, even thoughts.

"I can almost believe that you *were* born in 2003. But how did you get here?"

"Nina, you're not formulating the question correctly. The important thing is *why*, not *how*. I traveled into the past to meet you. I couldn't accept the fact decreed by fate that you were born forty years earlier than I. I saw your picture in an old family album at my Grandmother's and did everything I could so we could meet. As you see, I succeeded."

"Why?"

"Again you're not formulating the question correctly. Why do Pushkin or Shakespeare talk to us? Long ago people found a means of communicating with other generations. They called this invention the written language. Unfortunately it was not a total success: Pushkin can talk to us but we can't talk to him. In the ISFT, they've found a way to talk to Pushkin and Shakespeare—not across the void of centuries, but as first-hand, just as I am now speaking with you. And so I exist simultaneously now, and in my own century."

"How do you do it?"

"Again the wrong question. Remember: in order for me to answer you, I'll have to recall that which hasn't been and is not, but is yet to be, isn't that right? But instead of a memory it's a dream. . . . Do you want me to dream?"

"Yes," answered Nina. "I adore listening to your dreams."
The car swerved sharply, slowed and stopped.
"Get out!" said the driver.
"Surely we haven't arrived," Nina said in astonishment.
"It doesn't matter. Get out! I won't take you any farther."
"Did you run out of gas?"
"I have more than enough gas. Now, get out! Dream somewhere else, not in my taxi. I can't stand dreamers."

5

They settled in Nina's room. They certainly couldn't live in the garden where Oblakov had stood waiting for her.

From her window, Nina could see only a vacant lot where there had been a garden before. She know Oblakov was responsible for the change. He wasn't home yet, and she guessed that he had turned himself into a garden and was now standing under her window holding thick branches, full of leaves and the smell of late spring.

But then one day the garden disappeared. In its place once again there was the vacant lot with a lone, dejected salesman taking in empty bottles. Nina assumed that Oblakov had tired of standing under the window and that soon she would hear his footseps on the stairs.

The other tenants didn't know that their garden was a man, and had been overjoyed when they suddenly found a garden in the lot. They thought that an unusually gifted gardener was in charge of the city's gardens and parks, and that he wanted to show off his skill. They were very annoyed when the garden dissappeared. This seemed unnatural and illegal to them, in short a criminal and punishable act. They were just about to file a complaint with the authorities when a certain respected and sensible old man pointed out to them that the sequence of events was quite reasonable.

"Why, it was a piece of scenery," he said.
"And where has it gone?"
"They took it away."

"Why?"

"They used it for a key scene in a film. And then they took it away to save money. The woods were not real. You have to understand that."

Nina pleaded with Oblakov to turn into a garden only at night to avoid alarming people. He agreed unwillingly, for he preferred to sleep at night.

Their life passed like that of most newlyweds. They missed each other even when separated for a single hour. They ate lunch and dinner together in a small restaurant called 'The Deck.' The restaurant somehow seemed very much like a ship on a voyage through unfamiliar seas, with its little tables with white tablecloths, and pretty waitresses who refused tips.

Sid and Nina were like all newlyweds, but, with one exception: Oblakov's strange habit of recalling his future in contrast to most people, who remember their past.

Nina was fascinated with his tales of the future. Oblakov described it not as if it was still to come, but as a fascinating history replete with details.

"And you really were there?" Nina would say, at times doubtfully.

"I was," he would answer thoughtfully and quietly.

"But why do you speak of it so sadly? Are you sorry that you're with me in this century? Do you want to return? Have you forgotten the way?"

"You have not formulated the question correctly. There's no logic in it. There are no roads to where I came from."

"Explain it, Sid,"

"I can't, not just yet."

6

The sociologist would come to them with a crammed portfolio. He had a concerned expression on his face. In his portfolio were a large number of questionnaires, containing a multitude of questions.

The sociologist's questionnaires were like a trap, a sort of intellectual noose with which he sought to catch the psychological essence of the creative process. The sociologist moved toward this aim unhurriedly—step by step, like a savage hunter stealing his way towards a water hole frequented by the sensitive, timid animals of the Stone Age.

"Have you considered the possibility that you may be having hallucinations, if only during the time you and the garden become one and the same thing?"

"Not exactly. I really am able to achieve the transformation."

"Can you describe your condition on such an occasion?"

"I can."

"Be as explicit as possible," said the sociologist, in the tone of a man simultaneously playing the roles of physician and state prosecuter.

"I go out into the vacant lot under the window and begin to turn into a garden. I try to do it all at once so that no one will notice that I am becoming a tree. Usually I succeed, but one day not long ago the yardkeeper's wife happened to look out just at the wrong moment. 'Look, look! at what is happening to that man!' An excited crowd gathered but the sensible old pensioneer saved the day.

"You must understand: it's quite simple," he said to the crowd. "This is a filming. The actor is playing a role in a fairy tale. They'll shoot it and everything will go back to normal!"

"That's not it," interrupted the sociologist." You are describing how other people react to your condition. The opinions of others don't concern me now. I'm only interested in what you feel. Describe your psychological condition."

"My psychological condition," said Oblakov," is similar to that in a poem. I feel that the world and I are one. Just like in a good poem where there are no logical barriers between occurances. Internal events flow as freely as a river."

"Are you being creative during those moments?" asked the sociologist.

"It isn't that I am being creative—something stronger than myself is swaying me."

"You're avoiding my question. I want to know what kind of sensations you experience. Does it hurt, or are your sensations pleasant? Are you depressed, or relaxed? Do you feel exhausted?"

"I fell like a garden where the trees stand for decades, sometimes even for centuries. It's hardly likely they want to change position either to sit or lie down. They stand. I also stand. But unlike them, I can leave. The consciousness that I'm not tied to the soil plays its part."

"We don't understand each other," said the irritated sociologist. "You're avoiding my questions and my iron logic. Rest a while. Have a cigarette. Sit in complete peace for about ten minutes and collect your thoughts."

The sociologist opened his notebook and wrote:

"Overindulgence in metaphysical speech. Simultaneity of sensations. Perceives the world around him too concretely. Akin to hallucination. Possible that Oblakov is in the strange state between illusion and reality."

The sociologist sighed and closed the notebook.

7

In the course of just one year together, great changes took place in the lives of the Oblakovs. In the first place, he stopped turning into a garden. Little by little he forgot how to. Finally, he completely got out of the habit. Secondly, he stopped reminiscing about the twenty first century. His recollections moved from the future into the past and became not unlike an old family album. Neither his pictures nor his water colors startled Nina or her friends with their earlier freshness and novelty. They were exhibited for sale in the gallery on Nevsky Prospect and are still hanging there although their prices are much more than is reasonable!

The manager told Nina: "People are spoiled nowadays.

Everyone is demanding works by celebrities. And where can such work be found? We are overstocked to the tune of several million rubles. Your husband's pictures are only a drop in the bucket."

His words upset Nina, but she didn't say a thing to Sid who was sleeping peacefully when she returned home. Very quietly, on tip-toe so as not to awaken him, Nina gathered up some empty bottles, put them in a bag, and went to the vacant lot to the booth of the bottle-collector. The sensible old pensioneer was warming himself on a bench. Beside him sat the middle-aged, arrogant woman, the former beauty who ran the theater buffet during intermissions. She was complaining to the old man, "The vacant lot is still drab. At least they could have planted trees and flowers. I've dreamed of that for a long time."

"And what if they did," objected the pensioneer. "We can't wait till the trees grow. The process takes too much time."

Nina heard the pensioneer's bitter words when she gave the man her bottles, and for some reason these words upset her. It wasn't only that she was sorry the old man couldn't see the garden, but that her own life with Oblakov, which had begun so unusually, like a fairy-tale, had become very ordinary.

Upon returning home, Nina saw that Sidney was up and busy painting. He was doing a picture from the life of some sorcerers who were taught how to perform miracles. The sorcerers on his picture looked rather prosaic, and for some reason or other resembled the gloomy man from the booth who took in empty bottles.

Nina asked timidly: "Sid, why do your sorcerers resemble that bottle-collecter?"

Nina hoped that Sid would answer: "You have incorrectly formulated your question," but Oblakov had long since lost interest in logic. He yawned and answered, "I've forgotten how to work without a model. I don't trust fantasy.

Fantasy could carry me away from life to God knows where."

"But these are sorcerers!"

"So what? They're of no use to me. That man in the booth does a useful and interesting job—he buys up empty bottles."

Oblakov's words sounded logical and Nina couldn't find anything to say in reply.

"Sidney," she asked quietly, "Couldn't you turn into a garden for just half an hour?"

"Why?"

"I'd really like you to."

"Ridiculous! An idle game. To make such demands. It isn't ethical."

Nina waited while Oblakov washed a brush and put it on the window sill to dry. Then they went for dinner at 'The Deck.'

The restaurant no longer resembled a ship on a voyage to nowhere; rather as befitted a restaurant, it stayed solidly in place. The tablecloths were no longer remarkable for their whiteness and the waitresses served them without a smile.

"Sidney," Nina asked quietly, "Did you go to see the officer in the passport office?"

"Yes," he replied lazily.

"Why?"

"What do you mean: why? I can't go around with a passport indicating that I was born in 2003! According to my document I don't exist. Where's the logic?"

"Your being born in a future century really pleased me, Sidney. And it made me happy to know that you could become a garden."

"That was preposterous, Nina. Absurd."

"I don't know; but when you used to turn into a garden, you were a different man; and your pictures reflected it. It is as though you are someone else now."

8

The sociologist came again; this time without his portfolio and papers. He was very upset.

"Sidney Nikolaevich," said the sociologist, not hiding his anxiety. "I learned from your wife several days ago that you have ceased turning into a garden."

"I gave it up."

"Why?"

"My turning or not turning into a garden denies causality by my very action in so doing. It's illogical. It's impossible to explain from a scientific point of view to you in your time."

"You're repeating the very words that I used when analyzing you from a psychological point of view."

"Precisely! I took your advice. I began to conduct myself in a completely ordinary way, just like everyone else."

"You couldn't, by any chance, turn into a garden for just ten minutes? Please do it for me. I carelessly published an article about your peculiarities in a popular scientific journal. A committee has been appointed to verify my experiment."

"Your experiment?"

"Well, not mine, of course, yours. . . . That is, they want to verify your proclivity for semimorphism. Tonight a special commission will arrive to acquaint themselves with your special capacity."

"I've lost it. I've grown unused to it. It's possible that I can't do it without practice."

"Well, then practice! I'll make a note of the time." The sociologist looked at his watch.

Lazily, Oblakov went out to the vacant lot. Suddenly it grew dark. Branches sprang up from the empty spot and a garden shut out the sky. The smell of lilac and moist leaves wafted in through the windows.

"Tremendous!" the sociologist cried to Nina. "He did it! It worked! Look! It really is a most extraordinary phenomenon. I don't know, though, how to validate it theoretically. Let's go down and walk near the trees; we'll breathe the fresh air and ponder this inexplicable fact of spiritual and physical semimorphism."

Nina and the sociologist went down to the garden.

On the bench sat the former beauty, the theater buffet proprietress, and the old pensioneer. The former beauty said delightedly:

"How quickly they've learned to grow trees! In the morning this was only a vacant lot and now look how luxuriant the garden is!"

"It's not real," objected the old man. "It's only scenery. They'll come, shoot their film and take it away. You must understand that."

. . . Nina waited all day, then all night and through the next morning. Again twilight fell, but the garden remained standing on the vacant lot.

Translated by NATASHA S. GREEN.

Human Frailty

A. XLEBNIKOV

THERE WASN'T time to be frightened. The walls of the cabin disintegrated. A chasm suddenly opened up, and the frozen steam in the cabin created a "white explosion," which ripped into the cosmic vacuum. With a powerful push, Dana was swept away from the ship into the black emptiness. As she fell, she kept turning around and around, but to her scrambled sense it seemed that flashing red, yellow and violet stars were spinning about her, while she herself was motionless.

Somewhere in the distance, her ship rushed by, casting a barely discernable shadow upon the bright field of stars. . . . The ship's lights blazed like rasberry threads of lightning and vanished.

Dana continued to fall, a lone and helpless speck condemned to a speedy death.

"Lat," screamed the girl. "Lat, I've been ejected into space."

"Don't lose courage. Dana," came the imperturbable voice of the captain. "Just hang on. GEM will save us."

"Lat, where are you?"

"Not far from you."

"What happened?"

"A meteorite struck us. Probably antimatter. It punched a hole through both hulls." Silence followed.

"Lat, talk, say just anything, anything at all, keep talking," she beseeched. Dana was floating in bottomless space and the voice of the captain, her Lat, had become her sole link to reality, to the world of the living.

"Dana, when we get back to Earth, will you be able to pass the test on spaceship cybernetics even though your field is biology?" the captain asked quickly.

"I can."

"Bio-cybernetics is an unbeatable combination. But don't let it go to your head or, before you know it, you'll be transferred from the mineral carrier to some passenger liner."

"Lat, you're not lying? You're sure we'll return to earth?"

"Of course. The 'little pikes' are busy trying to locate us right now," the captain lied.

The astronauts had nicknamed the small rescue rocket *The Pike* because of its ability to trace down and "swallow" a man in space. Unfortunately it had just enough power to carry one person straight back to the mother ship."

The mineral carrier *Chrystal* had two *Pikes,* one for each crew member. Only the captain knew that one of the launching pads was located just beneath the smashed compartment.

"They'll find us in a few minutes," came the calm but thickly muffled voice of the captain.

"Lat! why can I barely hear you?"

"Don't worry. When we were tossed out of the ship we were propelled in different directions."

"Lat, can't you come closer to me?"

"No, there was no time to attach a propulsion unit to my suit. GEM sounded the alarm too late. Thank God we managed to get into space suits. . . . Dana, do you hear me?" The captain's voice was no louder than a whisper.

"Yes, yes."

"We're almost too far apart to hear each other. Our communications are breaking down, but don't be alarmed! Is your radio beacon working?"

"Yes, yes, it is."

"Hang on. Be brave. . . . Good. . . . ", The captain's

voice was cut off. The incessant sound of static, the language of the stars, poured into her earphones.

In the damaged compartment, the remains of the "white explosion" hadn't yet cleared when the patching film began to bind the ship's wound. The robot-reconnoiterers scurried along the exterior of the hull, determining the character and extent of the damage. Robot-electricians began to stir in their compartments, preparing for speedy action.

GEM, the ship's central electronic computer, worked with perfect precision and lightning speed. Electric impulses scattered throughout the ship forwarded the findings to the analytic section.

GEM discovered at once that both crew members had left the ship under abnormal circumstances, and therefore, needed emergency assistance. GEM also learned that one *Pike* had been destroyed but that the second was perfectly operational. GEM commanded that the hatch be opened. The undamaged *"Pike"* moved out of its nest; the whiskerlike antennae quivered and its small electronic brain came to life.

There were two objects in the void to be saved. The *Pike* radioed GEM for instruction.

"The captain first. If impossible, the biologist," was GEM's unavoidable decision. Its pre-set program read simply: "All effort is to be directed toward the prevention of danger to the ship and the return to normal functioning of all its systems." Logically, the captain-cyberneticist was to come first.

"Open your mouth, open your mouth, open your mouth. . . ."

Dana came to in the ship's infirmary.

"Lat!" she called.

A metal hand gently pressed a bottle to her lips.

"You must drink, you must drink, you must drink," monotonously muttered the robot-orderly.

"Lat!" she screamed, pushing the drink aside.

"Don't be upset, don't be upset," repeated the robot.

"Connect me with GEM."

"First—rest, business—later, business—later. . . . "

"I order you!"

The robot obeyed. A green eye lit up on the half globe of his head.

"GEM here."

"Where's the captain?"

"The captain perished."

"It's not true! We have two *Pikes*.'

"GEM never lies. There was only one undamaged *Pike* after the collision."

"Why was I saved and not the captain?"

"The captain turned off his radio beacon."

"Why did he do that?" Dana sobbed.

"There is only one explanation: human frailty. Robots would never act that way," GEM answered calmly.

Dana buried her head in the pillow and wept.

Translated by NATASHA S. GREEN.

A Modest Genius
A Fairy-Tale for Grown-Ups

VADIM SHEFNER

SERGEI KLADEZEV was born on Vasilyevsky Island, in Leningrad. From the first he was a strange child. At an age when others were making sand pies, he used the sand for a drawing board to trace parts of queer machines. In the second form at school he constructed a portable gadget fed from a flash-lamp battery which would tell any pupil how many bad marks he would get that week. But the grown-ups took it away. It was not pedagogically correct, they said.

After finishing general school, Sergei entered an electrochemical technical school. There were plenty of pretty girls training with him, but Sergei was unimpressed—perhaps familiarity bred indifference. One June day, however, he hired a boat and rowed along the Nevka to the gulf. By Volny Island he saw two girls in trouble: they had gone aground in the shallows and broken an oar in their efforts to get clear. He helped them get back and turn in the boat, and the acquaintance continued. Both of them lived on Vasilyevsky Island, Svetlana on the Sixth Line and Lusya on the Eleventh.

Lusya was then taking a typing course; Svetlana was not learning anything. She said she'd had enough of that at school, thank you. Besides, her parents were well-off and were beginning to say it was high time she got married.

At first Sergei liked Lusya the best, but he didn't know

how to approach her. She was so pretty, and modest, and bashful; she tried so hard to keep in the background that she made Sergei feel bashful too. But Svetlana, now—that was quite a different matter. She was gay and forthcoming, a girl to catch anyone's eye, and Sergei felt quite at ease with her, although by nature he was rather shy.

A year later, in July, Sergei went to stay with a friend in Rozhdestvenka and, lo and behold, Svetlana too had come to stay with relatives. It was the merest coincidence, but to Sergei it seemed like fate. Every day he went with Svetlana into the woods or on the lake. Soon he felt that without her life would be void of all meaning.

Svetlana, however, didn't quite see it that way. She thought him terribly ordinary. Svetlana dreamed of a husband who would be exceptional. But she went with Sergei to the woods and on the lake because, after all, you have to have *somebody,* now don't you?

One evening they stood on the lake shore, with the moon sending a track of silver to their feet, like a carpet woven by naiads. The water was smooth and the only sound was the trill of a nightingale in the wild lilac bushes on the far side of the lake.

"How lovely it is," sighed Sergei, "and so quiet."

"Yes, it's all right," Svetlana answered, "quite a fine view. I'd like to gather some of those lilacs but it's a long way round by the shore, and there isn't a boat anywhere near. And you can't run across a lake."

They returned home. But Sergei did not sleep, he spent the whole night drawing diagrams and making calculations. In the morning he went to the city and spent two days there. He came back carrying a bundle.

He took it with him when they went down to the lake side that evening. By the water's edge he unrolled it and disclosed two pairs of very special skates, on which one could glide over the water.

"Here, fasten on these water skates," he told Svetlana, "I invented them for you."

They fastened on the skates and glided easily over the water to the farther bank. The skates moved splendidly on the water. They broke off some of the best lilacs and then skated on the lake in the moonlight for a long time, carrying the flowers.

This now became their favorite evening occupation. They would race over the smooth surface on the swift water skates, leaving only a faint narrow track that soon smoothed over.

One evening, in the middle of the lake, Sergei came to a sudden stop. Svetlana slowed down and returned to him.

"Sveta, do you know?" said Sergei.

"No—what is it?"

"You know, Svetlana, I—love you."

"Oh bother, now you've spoiled everything."

"Don't you like me even a little bit, then?" Sergei asked.

"Oh, you're all right, only my ideal is quite different. I can only love a really exceptional man. And you—you're just ordinary, I have to be honest about it."

"Yes, of course, you have to be honest," said Sergei sadly.

Silently they returned to the bank, and the next day Sergei went back to the city. For some time he was in a bad way. He got thin, he tramped the streets restlessly, or went outside the city to tramp the countryside. But in the evenings he busied himself in his small laboratory workshop at home.

One day he met Lusya on the embankment, by the Sphinxes. He could see she was pleased to see him.

"What are you doing here, Sergei?" she asked.

"Just taking a walk. It's holidays, after all."

"I'm just taking a walk, too," said Lusya. "Look—why shouldn't we go to the park?" she added and blushed.

They went together to Elagin Island and strolled up and down the paths for a long time together. After that they met a number of times to stroll about the town. It was pleasant, being together.

One day when they were planning to go to Pavlovsk, Lusya called for Sergei.

"Goodness, what a mess!" she cried, looking around his room. "All those retorts and test tubes and queer-looking things—what are they all for?"

"Oh, I just like to fool about with inventing this and that".

"I never thought," Lusya marvelled. "Perhaps you could repair my typewriter? I bought it second-hand, it's rather old and the tape sometimes sticks."

"All right, I'll come in and take a look at it."

"What's that?" Lusya's eyes had been busy. "That's a queer sort of camera, I've never seen one like it."

"It's just an ordinary FED camera with a special attachment I've just made. With this gadget you can photograph forward. You direct it at the square you want to see in the future and snap the shutter. But my attachment's still imperfect, it won't go more than three years ahead."

"But three years—that's a lot! You've made a tremendous discovery!

"Oh, tremendous—!" Sergei gave a deprecating gesture. "It's still very crude."

"Have you any pictures?"

"Yes. I took some outside the city a few days ago." From a drawer in his writing table Sergei drew out several 9 by 12 centimeter photographs.

"Look, I snapped a birch tree by the meadow as it is now, without the attachment. And here's the tree as it will be in two years' time."

"It's grown a bit," said Lusya.

"But now look—in three years," said Sergei.

"Why, it isn't here at all,?" cried Lusya, surprised. "Just a stump and a hole beside it, a kind of crater. And look, there, in the distance, soldiers running, crouching. And they've got queer uniforms, too. I don't understand."

"I was surprised myself, when I printed it," Sergei admitted. "I suppose it's some sort of manoeuvres."

"You know, Sergei, I think you ought to burn that print. It may be a military secret. Supposing it fell into the hands of a foreign spy!"

"You're right, Lusya," said Sergei. "You know, I never thought of that!"

He tore up the print, threw it into a stove already stuffed with rubbish, and set a match to the lot.

"Now my mind's at ease," said Lusya. "Sergei, photograph me, the way I'll be in a year. In that armchair by the window."

"But the camera takes only the place it's directed at and what'll be there. If you won't be sitting in that chair in a year's time, then you won't appear at all."

"Take me, just the same. Perhaps I shall be in that chair, in exactly a year, at this time."

He photographed the chair with Lusya in it, but a year ahead.

"I'll develop it and take a print at once," he said. "The bathroom's free just now."

When the film was developed Lusya picked it up by the edge and peered at the last picture. Of course, a negative can be misleading, but it seemed to be somebody else sitting there. And she did so want it to be *her*, sitting there in a year's time. It must be me, she decided. It's just a bad picture.

As soon as the film was dry they went into the bathroom where Sergei had a red lamp. He placed the film in the enlarger, switched it on and made the print. He quickly placed the paper in the developer. There was the armchair. And a strange woman was sitting in it. She was embroidering a big cat in satin stitch. The cat was nearly finished, only the tail was lacking.

"But that's not me," said Lusya, disappointed. "It's somebody quite different."

"No, it's not you," Sergei agreed. "But I don't know who it is, I've never seen that woman in my life."

"Sergei, it's time for me to be getting home," said Lusya.

"And you needn't bother to come. I'll take my typewriter to a repair shop."

"Let me see you home, at least."

"No, Sergei, I'd rather you didn't. I don't want to be in your way. . . ." The next moment she was gone.

My inventions don't seem to bring me any luck, thought Sergei. He picked up a hammer and brought it down with a will on his camera attachment.

A month later, as Sergei Kladezev strolled along Grand Avenue, he saw a young woman on a seat and recognized her as the stranger in his photograph.

"Could you tell me the time?" she asked.

Sergei could, and did. He sat down on the bench. They began to talk about the Leningrad weather, and gradually passed on to other things. Her name was Tamara. The next time they met was not by accident. They began to see each other more frequently, and in due course they married. Then came a son whom Tamara called Alfred.

Tamara turned out to be a dull woman to live with. She was not interested in anything except sitting in her chair by the window embroidering cats, swans, and deer which she then hung proudly on the walls. She had no particular feeling for Sergei, she had married him simply because he had a good room and because she was soon to graduate the horse-breeding college and did not want to be assigned to a job somewhere out in the country; as a married woman the college had no right to send her away.

Being such colossal dullness herself, Tamara naturally regarded Sergei as dull, uninteresting, and insignificant. She did not like his absorption in his inventions; she thought it all a foolish waste of time.

Finding himself short of space in the room, Sergei constructed his LAGA—Local Anti-Gravitation Apparatus—which enabled him to work on the ceiling. He spread flooring, fixed up a workbench and brought up all his tools. To keep the wall clean, he made a narrow linoleum path up it. So now the floor was his wife's, and the ceiling was Sergei's workshop and lab.

Tamara, however, was still not pleased. She was afraid they might have to pay double rent for this increased space. Besides, she felt it was unfitting for her husband to walk about on the ceiling like a fly.

"If only out of respect for my education and my culture, you should not live upside down," she said from her chair below. "Oh dear, why must I have such an infliction? Other women have proper, respectable husbands, and I have to draw an oddity, no good to anyone!"

When he came home from work (he was now technical controller at Transenergoaccounts) Sergei swallowed down his dinner and then went up the wall to his ceiling, except for those days when Tamara's eternal nagging got too much for him; then he would go out and walk about the streets, or go outside the city to stretch his legs better. He developed such good walking legs that he thought nothing of going as far as Pavlovsk or Fox's Nose.

One day, at the corner of Eighth Line and Central, he met Svetlana.

"I'm married now, and my husband is a most exceptional man," Svetlana told him almost before greeting him. "My Petya's a *real* inventor! For the present he's still junior inventor in the research office of "Everything for Everyday," but he'll soon be promoted to intermediate grade. My Petya's patented an invention already—the "Don't Filch' soap."

"What's that?" asked Sergei.

"The idea's very simple—but then, genius always is simple, isn't it? "Don't Filch" is ordinary toilet soap, with a briquette of indelible Indian ink in the middle. If somebody —well, maybe your neighbor in a communal flat—takes that soap and starts to use it, he'll be blackened both morally and physically."

"But what if nobody filches it?" asked Sergei.

"Don't ask silly questions!" Svetlana snapped. "You're just envious, that's all!"

"Do you ever see Lusya?" asked Sergei. "How is she?"

"Oh, just the same as ever. I keep advising her to find some suitable, exceptional man and marry him, but she doesn't say anything. Apparently she wants to remain an old maid."

The war started soon afterwards, Tamara and the child evacuated, and Sergei Kladezev went to the front. He began as junior infantry lieutenant, and finished the war a senior lieutenant. As soon as it ended he returned to Leningrad, exchanged his uniform for civvies and went back to work at Transenergoaccounts. Then Tamara and Alfred came back and life slipped back into the old groove.

The years passed. Alfred grew up, finished school, and enrolled in a reduced brief course for hotel managers. Then he went south and found a position in a hotel.

Tamara still embroidered cats, swans, and deer. She was duller than ever, and nagged more. In addition, she had met a retired director, a bachelor, and threatened to leave her husband for the director if Sergei didn't learn sense and drop his idiotic inventions.

Svetlana was still highly pleased with her Petya. Petya was getting on in the world. He was now intermediate-grade inventor. He had even invented square spokes for bicycles instead of round ones. Svetlana was terribly proud of him.

Lusya still lived on Vasilyevsky Island. She was a typist in the Piano Spare Parts Office, where they were planned and designed. She had not married. And she often remembered Sergei. One day she saw him in the distance but kept away. He was walking along the Seventh Line towards the Baltic cinema with his wife—Lusya at once recognized the woman from the photograph.

Sergei often remembered Lusya, too. To drive her out of his mind, he concentrated on new inventions. He always thought them too crude and imperfect, however, to be subjected to the scrutiny of the inventions office. He invented, for instance, a Squabble Meter and Cut-Out and set up in the kitchen of the communal flat where he lived. The gadget had a scale of twenty divisions and recorded the mood of tenants and the intensiveness of squabbles if they arose. With the first snappish word the arrow began to tremble and move up the scale, gradually approaching a red line. When it came to this, it switched on the Squabble Cut-Out. Quiet, soothing music began; an automatic spray filled the air with tincture of valerian and White Night perfume, while a comical gleaming mannikin appeared on the screen, bowed and said, "Live in peace, dear people! Live in peace!" In this way the squabble was stopped at its outset, and all the neighbors were grateful to Sergei for his modest invention.

Sergei also invented plane optics. After treating a piece of window glass by his method, he gave it the qualities of a lens of tremendous power. He placed the glass in the window of his room and was able to observe the Martian canals, lunar craters, and Venusian storms. When Tamara really got under his skin too badly, he would gaze upon distant worlds and be comforted.

Actually, his life was not very gay. Neither Tamara nor Alfred made his life any happier.

When Alfred came to Leningrad, his main attention and conversation was for Tamara.

"Well, how are you getting along?" he asked her.

"How do you think? My only joy is my art. Look at the deer I'm embroidering."

"That's a fine deer. Looks really alive," said Alfred. "And the antlers he's got! If I'd antlers like that, I'd go far."

"Your father's got no feeling for art. All he wants is to invent. He'll never go far."

"At least he doesn't drink, give him his due," her son consoled her cheerfully. "Of course, he isn't getting ahead very well, but maybe he'll take a hold of himself yet. When I look at the people who stay in the hotel, and think of father, it makes me sick. A chief supplies agent, or a foreigner, or a scientist. A little while ago there was a big scholar in a deluxe suite; he was writing an autobiography of Pushkin. He'd got a country house and a fine car, too."

"What's the use of me thinking of country houses, with a husband like I've got," Tamara whined dismally. "I'm tired of him! I want a divorce."

"Have you anyone else in mind?"

"There's a manager, retired. A bachelor. And he's got a soul for art. I gave him a swan I'd embroidered, and he was as pleased as a child. I'd be all right with one like that."

"What was he manager of? Not a hotel?"

"No, a cemetery. A serious man. Tactful."

"Yes. The proper thing, in his work," her son agreed.

Then came a day in June when Sergei Kladezev worked all evening on a new invention, worked until very late without realizing how the time was going. When he went to bed he forgot to set his alarm clock, and overslept. He would be late for work anyway, so he decided not to go at all. It was his first and last day missed.

"You'll ruin yourself yet with your inventions," Tamara nagged. "If you missed your day's work for something useful—! Sensible people make money on the side, they grow strawberries and sell them, but you—there's as much good to be got from you as eggs from a cock!"

"Don't be so upset, Tamara, everything'll be all right," said Sergei mildly. "I'll soon have my holidays and then we'll take a trip down the Volga."

"I don't want any of your cheap trips!" Tamara screamed. "You'd do better to take a trip behind your own back and hear what people say about you! They just laugh at you for a fool!"

Angrily she snatched an embroidered cat off the wall and marched off.

Left alone, Sergei pondered.

He pondered for a long time, and at last decided to take a trip behind his own back, as his wife advised.

He had long ago invented an Invisible Presence Device—IPD. Its radius was thirty-five kilometres, more he could not reach. Sergei had never used the IPD to observe life in the

city, for it was unpleasantly like eavesdropping. But sometimes he had trained it on the woods nearby to watch the
birds building their nests and listen to their singing.

Now he decided to use the IPD in the city. He plugged
it in, moved the distance adjustment knob and division and
directed the antenna towards the kitchen of the communal
apartment where he lived. The kitchen immediately flashed
up on the screen. Two women stood by the gas stove talking
about various things. Then one said, "Tamara's gone to her
director again. Shameless hussy!"

"I'm sorry for Sergei Vladimirovich," said the other.
"Such a good man, and ruined by that wife of his. The
brains he's got—!"

"You're right," said the first. "He must be a real clever
man, and a good man, too. Only he just hasn't any luck in
life."

Sergei switched off the IPD and sank into thought. He
remembered Lusya, and longed to see her, even if only for
a moment.

He switched on the device again and began to search
for Lusya's room on the sixth floor of the house of Eleventh
Line, Vasilyevsky Island. But perhaps she wasn't living there
any more, he thought suddenly. She might have got married
and moved away, or exchanged her room for something else.

Unknown rooms appeared on the screen, strange people,
fragments of other lives snatched for an instant from the
great city. And then he found Lusya's room. She was not
there, but it was her room. It had the same things in it, the
same picture on the wall. There was a typewriter on the
table. Sergei sighed with relief. Lusya must be at work, he
guessed.

Then he started tuning in to Svetlana's house—it would
be interesting to know how she was getting on. He found
her quite quickly. There were plenty of new things in the
apartment and Svetlana herself looked older, but quite
pleased with life.

The bell rang and Svetlana went to open the door.

"Why, Lusya, come in, it's a long time since you've been!" cried Svetlana.

"I just ran in for a moment, it's my dinner hour," said Lusya, and then Sergei saw her. She too had not got any younger in these years, but she was still sweet-faced and pleasant.

The two friends came back into the room and began to talk about this and that.

"You're not thinking of getting married even yet?" Svetlana asked suddenly. "You could still find some very respectable elderly man."

"No, I'm not looking for anybody," Lusya answered sadly. "The one I wanted married long ago."

"Are you still thinking of Sergei?" said Svetlana. "Whatever did you see in him? There's nothing exceptional about him. He'd never set the Neva on fire. Of course, he was a harmless sort of boy. He gave me some water skates, I remember. We skated on the lake with them. Nightingales were singing on the bank, everybody was asleep and we raced over the water—skated like professionals!"

"I never knew he'd made skates like that," said Lusya thoughfully. "Have you still got them?"

"No, of course not! My Petya sent them to the scrap metal collectors. He said they were just old rubbish. My Petya's a real inventor, he understands such things."

"Is Petya doing well?"

"Couldn't be better! Not long ago he designed his UMTAJO–1. It's a really bold flight of technological imagination."

"But what's an UMTAJO?"

"Universal Mechanical Tin and Jar Opener—that's what it is! Now housewives and bachelors will be rid of all the fuss of opening tins."

"Have you got one?" asked Lusya. "I'd like to see it."

"No, and I shan't have. It weighs five tons and needs a concrete foundation. And it'll cost four hundred thousand rubles."

"But what housewife can buy it, then?" Lusya wondered.

"Oh, how slow you are!" cried Svetlana. "It's not meant for each housewife to have one, there'll be one for a whole town. It'll be set up somewhere in the center—on Nevsky Prospekt, say. And there a MOS will be opened—a Main Opening Shop. It'll be very convenient. Suppose, say, you have unexpected visitors and want to open a tin of sardines or something. You don't need to jab with a tin opener or make any physical effort. You simply take your tin or jar, and go out to the MOS. You hand over your tin or jar to a reception clerk, pay five kopecks and get a receipt. The reception clerk labels your tin or jar and puts it on a conveyor. And you go into the waiting room, settle down in a chair and watch a short film about making preserves . . In a little while you're called to a window, hand over your receipt, get your opened tin or jar and go home with it."

"And is this really going to be done?" asked Lusya.

"Petya hopes for it," Svetlana answered. "But he's got a lot of enemies and maligners, especially recently, and they try to block his inventions. They're just envious, that's what it is. But Petya doesn't envy anybody because he knows he's exceptional. And he's fair-minded, too. There's one inventor he respects very much, the one who invented the "Bottoms Up" cork and got it brought into general use."

"But what's that—'Bottoms Up'?"

"Why, don't you know how vodka's corked nowadays?! It's a cap with a sort of tail at the side, made of soft metal. You pull the tail, the metal tears and your bottle's open. But you can't close it again, not with that cap, however much you try, so you have to drink all that's in the bottle. That's a soaring flight of technological thought, too."

"I like the idea of the water skates better," said Lusya musingly. "How I'd love to glide over the bay on them during the white nights!"

"You and those skates!" laughed Svetlana. "Petya and I wouldn't have them as a gift."

Sergei switched off his IPD again and once more plunged into thought. Then he came to a certain decision.

That evening Sergei Kladezev found his own pair of water skates at the bottom of an old suitcase. He filled the bath with water and tested them. They had not lost their water-repellant quality and could glide over the surface as smoothly as many years ago.

Till late that night he worked in his ceiling laboratory making a second pair, for Lusya.

The next day was Sunday. Sergei put on his best grey suit and wrapped both pairs of skates in newspaper. Then he slipped into his pocket a spray and a bottle of SAST (Super-Augmenter of Surface Tension). Clothes treated with this liquid would support a person upon the water.

Finally, Sergei opened a big cupboard where he kept his best inventions and took out his SEDAL (Solar-Energy Device, Application Limited). He had devoted a great deal of thought to this device at one time and considered it his most important idea. He had completed it two years ago, but had never yet employed it. The SEDAL could restore youth. But in these years Sergei had had no desire whatsoever for his own youth to be restored because that would mean restoring Tamara's too and starting life with her all over again. Sergei felt that one life with Tamara was more than enough. A second point was the amount of energy the device would require. It might even cause cosmic phenomena, and Sergei did not regard himself as sufficiently important for anything like that.

Now, however, after weighing everything, he decided to use it. So he took the SEDAL as well as the water skates and left the house.

He walked along his street and soon came to Central Avenue of Vasilyevsky Island. At the corner of the Fifth Line he bought a bottle of champagne and a box of chocolates and went on. At Eleventh Line he turned off and was soon standing before the house where Lusya lived. He climbed the familiar stairs and rang—two rings, one short.

Lusya opened the door.

"How are you, Lusya," he said. "It's a long time since we met."

"A very long time," Lusya answered. "But somehow, I've always known you'd come. And you have."

They went into Lusya's room; they drank champagne and recalled old times, many years ago.

"Oh, if only I could be young and start life all over again!" Lusya cried.

"That's quite possible," said Sergei and set his SEDAL on the table. It was about the size of a portable radio set. A thick cord emerged from it.

"Does it plug in? It won't cause a short-circuit, will it?" asked Lusya. "Our house went over to 220 volts not long ago."

"No, the SEDAL doesn't plug in," Sergei answered. "A thousand Dnieper power plants wouldn't be enough. It gets energy directly from the sun. Would you open the window?"

Lusya threw it open and Sergei carried the cord to the opening. It ended in a small concave mirror, and Sergei set that mirror on the sill so that it was directed at the sun.

Something crackled inside the device and the sun began to darken like a lamp when the current becomes weak. The room dimmed.

Lusya went to the window and looked out.

"Sergei, what's happening?" she marvelled. "It's like the beginning of an eclipse. All Vasilyevsky Island's in twilight. And farther away, too—it's getting dark everywhere."

"Dusk is falling now over all the earth, and on Mars, and on Venus," Sergei answered. "The device takes a lot of energy."

"A device like that would be no good for mass production," said Lusya. "Everybody would want to get their youth back, and it would always be dark."

"Yes," Sergei answered, "it's a once-only, single-person

device. I made it only for you and for your sake. And now sit down. We just sit here quietly."

They sat down on the old plush sofa, took hands and waited.

It became darker, as though night were falling. Street lamps went on, and windows lighted up. It was quite dark in the room, except for the cord which connected the mirror on the window-sill with SEDAL; it glimmered with a bluish light, and writhed and quivered like a pipe with liquid flowing through it at a terrific speed.

A sharp click sounded from the device, and a square window flew open in its side. A column of greenish light shot out. It was a column chopped off at the end, resting on space. It looked solid, but it was light. It began to extend until it reached the wall where a picture hung, a picture of a pig under an oak tree, an illustration to one of Krylov's fables. In an instant the pig had turned into a piglet and the spreading oak into a sapling.

The ray moved hesitantly about the room as though blindly seeking Lusya and Sergei. Wherever it touched the wall the faded paper regained its former colors and looked like new. The elderly grey cat dozing on a chest of drawers became a kitten and began to chase its tail. A fly caught in the ray became a fly-grub and fell to the ground.

At last the ray drew near to Sergei and Lusya. It slid over their heads, their faces, their bodies and legs. Two pale semi-circles like halos rose over their heads.

"Oh—my head's tickling," laughed Lusya.

"Don't worry, try to stand it," said Sergei. "It's the grey hairs getting their color back. My head tickles, too."

"Oh!" Lusya gasped. "There's something hot in my mouth."

"Did you have gold crowns on your teeth?" asked Sergei. "Only two."

"Young teeth don't need crowns, they're dissolving into dust," Sergei explained. "Blow it out."

Lusya pursed her lips like an inexperienced smoker and blew out a mouthful of gold dust.

"The sofa feels as it it's rising up," she said suddenly.

"It's the springs. We're getting lighter. We've put on a little weight in these years."

"That's true, Sergei," Lusya agreed. "But now I feel so light—just as I did when I was twenty."

"And that's what you are now, twenty," said Sergei. "We've gone back to our youth."

That moment the SEDAL suddenly trembled, hummed and flashed. Then it vanished, leaving only a puff of pale-blue dust. At once it grew lighter. Drivers turned off their headlights; the street lamps went out; the windows darkened. And the sun shone again with all its June brightness.

Lusya rose, looked at herself in the mirror and smiled.

"Let's go out somewhere, Sergei," she said. "To Elagin Island, maybe."

When the quiet white night descended and the park emptied they came to the shore of the gulf. There was a flat calm, the sails of yachts stood motionless in the distance, by Volny Island. The water was mirrorlike, without a ripple.

"Just the right weather," said Sergei, unrolling the newspaper wrappings and took out the water skates. He helped Lusya fix them over her shoes, and then put on his own.

They stepped onto the water and glided lightly over the gulf. They passed yachts with men whistling for a wind, waved to them, and raced to Volny Island and the open sea. For a long time they skimmed to and fro until at last Sergei slowed down. Lusya in her turn slowed down and came close to him.

"You know what I want to say to you, Lusya?" Sergei began uncertainly.

"I know," Lusya answered. "And I love you, too. Now we'll always be together."

They kissed, and turned towards the shore.

The wind was rising now, and whipping up ripples and waves. Skating became difficult.

"What'll happen if I stumble and fall into the water?" asked Lusya.

"I'll fix everything right away so we won't drown," laughed Sergei.

From his pocket he took the spray and the bottle of liquid SAST. He sprayed Lusya's clothes and then his own.

"Now we can even sit down on the waves if we want," he said.

They sat down on a wave like on a bench of crystal, and put their arms round one another, and the wave carried them to the shore.

Translated by Eve Manning.

A Raid Takes Place
at Midnight*

ILYA VARSHAVSKY

PATRICK REID, chief of the Police Department, sat down in the armchair obligingly moved towards him and looked around. The white consoles with rows of buttons and varicolored lights somehow reminded him of an automatic cocktail shaker. The likeness of the computer center to a bar was further enhanced by two pert girl operators in white smocks sitting at the console. The girls had too much make-up on their faces, which Reid definitely did not like. But then, that went for the whole affair with the installation of the electronic machine. If the Interior Department paid less attention to the newspapers, there would have been no need at all to introduce all these new-fangled gadgets. Besides, in his fifty years with the police, Patrick Reid had learned that, whatever you did, if you were left with an unsolved crime on your hands, the papers were sure to raise a hue and cry about the police being bribed by the gangsters. Bribed! What the hell did they need to bribe for? Any gangster syndicate was better equipped than the police: armoured cars, helicopters, automatic weapons, teargas bombs, and most important, they were free to shoot when they wanted and at whom they wanted. Bribed! Mph!

David Logan was burning with impatience, but he was afraid of interrupting the chief's ruminations. You could tell

101

that the old man was highly skeptical of the whole thing from the way he pretended that it didn't concern him at all. Well, well, we'll see what he says when he gets the low-down. You don't have such a crime every day!

Reid took a pipe out of his pocket and looked and looked about for a "No Smoking" sign.

"Here you are, sir!" Logan clicked a lighter.

"Thanks."

Reid puffed at his pipe for several minutes in silence. Logan made marks with a pencil on the perforated tape, watching the chief out of the corner of his eye.

"So you want to tell me," Reid finally broke the silence, "that this night the National Bank will be raided?"

"Yes, sir."

"Why today, and why the National Bank?"

"Here you are, sir." Logan handed Reid a sheet of paper. "The computer has analyzed all bank robberies over the last fifty years and extrapolated the data. And the next robbery—" Logan's pencil hovered over a dot on the broken curve, "the next robbery falls on today."

"Hmm. . . ." Reid pointed at the diagram. "Where does it say that it's the National Bank?"

"This follows from the theory of probability. The mathematical expectation. . . ."

The National Bank. Reid recalled the 1912 robbery. He had had his knee shot in a fierce gun battle, but had overtaken the robbers on his motorcycle. Bucolic times, those had been, when criminals operated in small gangs and were armed with old-fashioned Colts. Courage and prowess meant something then. But nowadays . . . . "Mathematical expectation," "correlation," Gaussian functions, punched cards. Good God! It was more like a mathematics class than a police force.

". . . Thus, there can be no doubt that Scoletti's gang. . . ."

"What's that?" Reid jerked back to reality.

"Scoletti's gang. It has the most modern safe-cracking

devices, and it hasn't carried out a major raid for a long time."

"Did the machine tell you about Scoletti?"

The machine considers that it will be Scoletti's gang. The probability is eighty-six percent."

Reid got up and walked over to the control console.

"Let's see how it works."

"Certainly. We can have it repeat all the basic computations."

"That's all right. I just wondered. So tonight Scoletti's gang will crack the safes of the National Bank?"

"Yes, sir."

"Well, I can only say I'm sorry for him."

"Why?"

"Because here's a raid being prepared: you and I know about it, the machine knows about it—only Scoletti doesn't suspect a thing!"

A sweet feeling of revenge swept through Logan. "That's where you're wrong, sir," he said maliciously. "Scoletti's gang has got itself exactly the same kind of machine, and you can be sure it'll tell him what to do."

Jean Bristeau had exchanged his university career for money, and he never regretted it. He felt the sober self-satisfaction of a man who has voluntarily given up the promise of heavenly bliss for the sinful delights of the earth. Nor did he experience any pangs of conscience for having handed over all his knowledge lock, stock and barrel, to a gangster syndicate. When all was said and done, a programmer was a programmer, and old man Scoletti paid ten times more than any aboveboard company ever would. Actually, it was like a game of chess. A tournament of electronic machines. Jean snorted and cast a sidelong glance at the fat old man, whose bodyguard was at the moment pouring out a second glass of hot milk from a thermos. Here was a scene the reporters would have scrambled for: Tony Scoletti, the menace of banks, sipping hot milk.

"Well, sonny," Scoletti said, placing his empty glass on

the computer console and turning to Bristeau. "So your for-tune-teller forecasts a good job for today?"

Bristeau made a face at the word "fortune-teller." No, sir, if you've gone and got yourself an electronic computer and decided to heed the voice of science, you ought to pick your expressions accordingly.

"I have succeeded," he said dryly, "in discovering a formula expressing the periodicity of band raids. Successful raids, of course," he added, picking up a wooden pointer. "On this diagram they are represented by the black circles. The red circles are raids computed according to my formula. The vertical positions of the circles correspond to their cash value, the horizontal, the date. You can see that the next major raid falls on today. I see no reason why we shouldn't take the goods."

"How much?"

"Forty million."

One of the bodyguards whistled. Scoletti turned around angrily. He hated sudden noises.

The syndicate boss sat still for a few minutes, puffing quietly, apparently weighing the proposition.

"What bank?"

"The National."

"Hmmm . . . ."

You could see that Scoletti was not too eager to tackle the National Bank, on which the syndicate had already twice drawn a blank. On the other hand, forty thousand grand was a sum well worth the risk of several casualties.

Bristeau knew the reason for Scoletti's hesitation, and decided to play his trump card.

"Of course, the whole operation will be planned by the machine."

The old man wavered. The one thing he never liked was shouldering the responsibility of planning a job. But if the machine did it . . . . Suddenly he remembered. "Wait a minute! They say old Reid's got a machine like this installed in his joint. What if it warns him?"

"So what?" Bristeau shrugged the objection aside. "We have the edge on him anyhow: we *know* he has a machine; *he* can only suspect we have one."

"Well?"

"It makes all the difference. The machine can draw up several variants of the job. Some may be better, others worse. Now suppose the cops' machine warns them of the possibility of a raid. Their next job will be to determine the syndicate that will undertake the raid, and the tactics it will employ. Taking the best variant as a basis, it will accordingly programme the best mode of action for the police."

"And catch us with our pants down."

"No, they won't!"

"How come?"

"Because, knowing this, we won't employ the best variant, but one of the other ones."

Scoletti wrinkled his nose. "Nuts, boy. All they'll do is ambush us in the bank and pick us off like chickens."

"That's where you're wrong," Bristeau objected. "Reid will never risk an ambush."

"Why not?"

"For purely psychological reasons."

"What do you know about a cop's psychology?" Scoletti grunted. "I know the old man for more than thirty years, and I can tell you he likes to strike for sure and he will set the trap."

Bristeau picked up a spool of punched tape from the console. "I may not know a cop's psychology, but the machine is capable of solving psychological problems, if it is duly programmed. And here is the solution of such a problem. Given: Reid is seventy-four. Some people in the Interior Department have long been wanting to get a younger and more pliable man in his place. Secondly, an ambush in the National Bank would require the consent of the Interior Department and have to be okayed by the Treasury. What has Reid to gain from laying an ambush? A purely tactical advantage. What does he stand to lose if something misfires? His reputation.

The papers will start shouting that the police can't deal with a gang of robbers even when it has advance knowledge of a raid. Reid will look even more foolish if he lays his ambush and there is no raid. The question is: Will Reid seek permission for an ambush, especially if he doesn't trust the machine too much? Of course not. See?"

Scoletti scratched his head. "Let's have a look at the variants," he said, settling down more comfortably.

"Well," said Reid, "your first variant is sure in Scoletti's style. Plenty of showmanship: armoured cars, fireworks, and the whole idea of blocking the area. But I can't see why he should stage a fake attack here." Reid's finger pointed at a street in the city centre. "Drawing a large police force here would make sense only if we knew of the raid in advance and decided to forestall it."

Logan could not conceal a triumphant smile. "Only in that case," he agreed. "Scoletti's sure we know his plans, and he's planning accordingly!"

"Sounds funny."

"There's nothing funny. The fact that the Police Department had installed a new electronic computer was publicized in all the papers. Do you imagine that the men in Scoletti's computer center are such fools as not to take account of our ability to forecast crimes? The police wouldn't get itself a machine only to improve its betting chances on the races."

Reid flushed. He liked to play the tote. It was one of his small weaknesses, which he tried to hide from his subordinates. "Well, what follows from this?" he inquired dryly.

"It follows that Scoletti will not employ variant number one, even though it is the best one from his point of view."

"Why not?"

"Precisely because it's the best one."

Reid knocked his pipe out, refilled it and, enveloped in clouds of blue smoke, pondered this piece of logic. Several minutes passed before he exclaimed happily: "By gosh, Dave, I think I've got it! You mean to say the syndicate not only suspects that we know about the raid but also that we know their plans?"

"That's just it. They know our machine has the same capabilities as theirs. In other words, we too have the raid plans, and in planning our counterblow we're bound to proceed from the ones most advantageous for Scoletti's gang."

"So they. . . ."

"So they will adopt the second best plan, which will come as a surprise to the police!"

"Whew!" Reid wiped his red neck with a checked handkerchief. "You mean we should. . . ."

". . . Should analyze plan number two," Logan broke in, and signalled to the two girls to set the machine going.

"I can't see why you're against this variant," Bristeau said.

"Because it's nuts!" Scoletti's voice shook with anger. "You think if I've got half a dozen helicopters I can go around dropping thousand-pound bombs and landing paratroopers? You take me for the War Department? What's wrong with the first variant, I'd like to know?"

"Don't you see," Bristeau persisted, "that the advantage of the second variant is that, at least in the eyes of the police, it can't be carried out. Because where can we get aviation bombs?"

"That's just what I'm saying."

"But now imagine that we *have* got the bombs. The police will be totally unprepared for variant number two; because they think it can't be done, and they'll prepare for variant number one."

"Well?"

"Well, that means forty million will go over from the bank to our safes."

The mention of forty million made Scoletti ponder. He scratched the back of his head, then moved over a telephone and dialed a number. "Hullo, Pete? I need two thousand-

pound aviation bombs. This evening. What? O.K., let me
know."

"There you are," said Bristeau. "Nothing is too hard for
the Scoletti syndicate!"

"Wait till the bombs come. What if Pete can't get them?"

"In that case we have variant number three."

It was terribly hot in the control room of the Police
Department's computer center. The brush-work prettiness of
the girl operators melted in the streams of hot air rising
from the machine.

Reid and Logan bent over the console, which was littered
with scraps of paper tape.

"All right," Reid said in a hoarse voice, speaking above
the clatter of the automatic typewriter, "suppose Scoletti does
get a couple of discarded aviation bombs. It's hardly likely but
I'm ready to accept it as a working hypothesis."

"Aha, you see, you. . . ."

"Wait a moment, Dave. I say it only because in compari-
son with this digging a hundred-and-sixty foot tunnel, especially from the grounds of a foreign embassy, is just stark,
raving madness."

"Why?"

"Because, in the first place, digging a tunnel takes a lot
of time, and secondly, a foreign embassy. . . . It's crazy."

"But look here." Logan unfolded a plan on the desk.
"The embassy building is ideally located. A tunnel along
the shortest distance leads right into the bank's vault. Besides. . . ."

"For Christ's sake, who'll allow them to dig a tunnel
from there?" Reid exploded.

"We'll analyse this question separately," Logan said with
a wry smile. "I've already prepared the program."

"That's enough, kid!" Scoletti took his stockinged feet
off the console and stretched them out towards the bodyguard, who hastily picked up his shoes from the floor. "We're
wasting time. Your first variant suits me okay."

"Yes, but we've said it's the most dangerous one. If we go by it, we give the police the edge."

"Oh yeah? When do the cops expect the raid?"

"Today."

"Well, we make it tomorrow."

"Padre," Bristeau said awesomely, "that's not a head you've got but a computing machine. It gives us double the number of variants!"

"Well," said Logan, unbuttoning the collar of his sweat-drenched shirt, "variant number seven brings us back to variant number one. Gosh! Say, chief, why not just lay an ambush in the bank?"

"We can't, Dave. A thing like that could well spark a rush on the stock exchange. Any request for permission to lay an ambush will get known to the scribes, and then. . . ."

"Mm-yes. . . . I suppose you're right. Especially as variant number eight puts off the raid till tomorrow, and in that case. . . . Answer that telephone, somebody! It's been ringing for half an hour!"

One of the girls went over to the telephone. "Its for you," she said to Reid, covering the receiver with her hand.

"Say I'm busy."

"It's the duty officer. Says it's top urgent."

Reid took the receiver. "Hullo. Yes. When? All right. . . . No, better a motorcycle. I'll be right over."

Reid hung up and gave Logan a long, searching look. When he finally spoke his voice was strangely calm.

"You know Dave, you were right."

"About what?"

"The National Bank was robbed ten minutes ag ."

Logan blanched. "You don't mean Scoletti. . . ."

"I suppose Scoletti's got tied up with a damn fool like you. No, it looks like Silly Simms' work. He usually walks in brandishing a 1912 Colt and a tin can on a meat-grinder handle."

Translated by VLADIMIR TALMY.

A Farewell on the Shore

YEVGENY VOISKUNSKY AND
ISAI LUKODYANOV

> From time to time one comes across beings who seek to
> awake in others an awareness of the rustling, the mysterious
> whispering, of the unexplored.
> —*Alexander Green*

THE WHITE DIESEL ship slowly approached the rocky shore.

Gay and well-dressed, the passengers clustered on the
deck. They chattered and laughed in anticipation of the joys
of swimming and relaxing, and they admired the dolphins
which kept jumping out of the blue-green water.

Platonov was in no way distinguishable from the vaca-
tioners. He reflected a bit about this and smiled ironically
at his own joyless thoughts.

The *Feodor Chalyapin,* rounding the arm of the cape,
sailed into a wide bay, and all at once a town came into
view.

Platonov looked with curiosity at the yellow houses
spread out picturesquely along the rocks, and at the wild
tropical greenery. The white cone of a lighthouse at the end
of a breakwater was clearly imprinted against the azure sky.
Above the harbor and the glass cube of the marine station,
above the tiled roofs of the houses, trembled the haze of a
sultry day.

"Well, hello, old Kara-Buroon," thought Platonov, mentally addressing the city. Had he spoken his greeting aloud, it

would have sounded overly familiar, since he had never been in this place before.

Kara-Buroon lay on the site of an ancient Greek settlement. It had known flourishing times, with the rapid influx of wealth drawn from overseas trade, and times of decay, when trade declined and freight was carried to more thriving ports. Like mute witnesses to a long-gone age, tumbledown watchtowers rose on the rocky knolls above the town. Instead of muskets trained on the sea, the gay branches of wild nut trees peeped out from their loopholes.

Kara-Buroon was inaccessible by land, and could be reached only with difficulty from the sea—a fact which proved very important in the days of its heroic defense against the fascist landings during the Great Patriotic War.

But it was a long time ago that warships frequented the harbor of Kara-Buroon. Now its port welcomed only passenger vessels during the resort season—a season which amounted, however, to ten months of the year! Waves of tourists rolled into town. Busily clicking their photo and movie cameras, they crowded the electric train which carried them to Chalcedony Bay with its beautiful beaches, its multistoried boarding houses, solaria and aeraria, its dozens of cafes and snack-vending machines.

In Kara-Buroon lived employees of the district departments, doctors, and workers from the resort and the souvenir factory. A considerable part of the town's population was made up of retired navy men who spent their leisure time cultivating strawberries and fishing.

Here, too, lived Mikhail Levitsky, Platonov's nephew. They had not seen each other for thirty years. Mikhail had been quite a young boy then. All Platonov knew about his nephew was that he had become a doctor and had settled down in Kara-Buroon. What kind of man was he? Yanina, his late sister, had told Platonov once that Mikhail was a clever boy. But did he have the wisdom and tact to refrain from intrusive questions? For indeed, there is the wisdom of the head *and* the wisdom of the heart. Platonov, in the present situation, favored the second variety.

The *Feodor Chalyapin* slowly drew up to the harbor wall, and Platonov saw a gaily dressed crowd of welcomers. Somewhere among them was Mikhail Levitsky—the resort doctor, Yanina's son, the clever boy—Platonov's only surviving relative.

A noisy crowd of boys and girls with rucksacks on their shoulders pushed through the thick wall of passengers toward the gangplank. One of them, a lighthaired, sturdy fellow, a cabinmate of Platonov's, clapped him on the shoulder and said:

"Well, what do you say, will we see you in Chalcedony?"

"Certainly, you will," answered Platonov, thinking to himself, "We'll never see each other again, my friend."

And he mused further: "If I don't take a liking to my nephew, then the devil with him. Probably half the town rents out apartments here."

Platonov shied away from the loneliness of life in a hotel.

For Mikhail Levitsky it had been a troublesome day. Starting in the morning, an ordinary three-minute appointment had stretched into thirty-five minutes; after that, he had gone the rounds of the wards he supervised in the geriatric sanatorium "Longevity"; then had come his office hours.

Mikhail was a geriatrist, a specialist in the treatment of old people. He knew them well—their typical ailments, the changes that came with old age in the composition of their blood and cutaneous fat, and the quirks that make old people so difficult to live with. He had to spend more than an hour with a new patient—Mikhail had decided that their first concern should be her heart and circulatory system, but the patient insisted that they should rid her of her wrinkles without delay.

Toward two o'clock, he set aside his work and ran to the pier to meet his uncle. Of course he knew he had a maternal uncle by the name of Georgi Platonov, but he had never in his life been in touch with Platonov before receiving this telegram out of the blue. . . . "Meet me."

Mikhail stood beside the gangplank and looked sullenly around at the passengers from the *Chalyapin* disembarking into the pier. He didn't know what Platonov looked like, but correctly assumed that his uncle must be over seventy, not a bit less. If this foolish old man had only thought to send a phototelegram with his picture.... But that was unlikely. He knew old men well—their obstinacy and stinginess.

The passengers descended the gangplank in a solid stream, then they came in a thin trickle, and finally the gangplank was empty. Not one old, or even middle-aged looking man had passed by Mikhail.

He threw back his head and called out to a man in a white uniform cap, who was puffing away on a pipe.

"Is everybody off? Could someone be sleeping in his cabin?"

"We woke everyone up," answered the cap with dignity.

Mikhail turned around to leave and noticed a tall man of about forty standing next to him. The man's grey eyes looked out from beneath the visor of his cap at Mikhail calmly and just a little mockingly.

"You, too, seem to have missed your party," said Mikhail.

"Obviously, I haven't," answered the stranger. "You're Mikhail Levitsky, and you were supposed to meet your uncle, isn't that so?"

"True," said Mikhail in surprise. "Only we've missed each other. . . ."

"Not so," the stranger smiled. "Hello, nephew. I noticed right away that you resemble your mother."

"Pardon me. . . ! You are Georgi Platonov? But I thought you . . . "

"You're right, I'm indeed quite old. But as you can see, I have taken good care of myself. Is there a room at your house for me?"

"A room. . . ?" Mikhail was so flustered by his uncle's unexpectedly youthful looks that he didn't understand the meaning of his question right away. Then he caught on: "Yes, of course, your room is ready."

"Let's go then."

Platonov had two rather heavy suitcases. Mikhail reached out for the larger one, but his uncle gently pushed him aside:

'Take the other. No offense meant, but I'm somewhat stronger than you are."

They walked through the wide-open doors of the marine station over which hung a sign, "Welcome to Kara-Buroon," and came out onto the station square. Platonov stopped, pleasantly surprised. The palm trees stood like a green wall. To the left ran the quay, lined with smart-looking, gaily colored houses. Huge trees had woven a roof over the quay, and a deep blue shadow dappled with sunny patches darkened the asphalt. The street curved smoothly, following the line of the bay.

Beyond the boulevard the waterfront town climbed precipitously up the rocky hill. Platonov gazed curiously at the arched foot bridges and stone stairways, the toy cars of the furnicular railways, the little bamboo grove on the slopes of one of the ravines. The red, yellow, and deep blue colors were bright and clear as a bell.

Yes, he had done the right thing by coming here. This lovely, strange city fully suited his purposes.

"Let's go on, Uncle Georgi," said Mikhail, pronouncing with some awkwardness the words, "Uncle Georgi."

He directed his new-found relative to the right—there stood an ancient arch, and beyond it a steep road, laid in flagstones. "Three Mile Way," read Platonov on the sign. Clumps of irrepressible grass had thrust up through the cracks between the flagstones. Mikhail, warming to his role as a guide, told how complicated it was to build in Kara-Buroon, pressed against the sea as it was by the rocks, and what enormous labor it had required to have water piping and a sewer system installed here.

They kept climbing higher. To the right, through the breaks in a grove of nut trees, shone the sea, laced with sunlight, and to the left the little yellow houses were engulfed by the green of their gardens. Mikhail broke out in a sweat.

His breath began to come in gasps from the climb, from the suitcase and from the fact that he was talking a lot. He looked out of the corner of his eye at Platonov. The latter walked with an even gait. The heavy suitcase apparently didn't bother him much. Seventy years and more? Well, if that was so, that he, Mikhail Levitsky, a specialist in old men, had never seen such a specimen before.

A procession was descending to meet him. To the song of violins and French horns and the rumble of a drum walked tanned boys and girls wearing garlands of red and white flowers.

"What's this?" asked Platonov, moving to the side of the road. "Not in honor of my arrival?"

"No," Mikhail answered seriously. "This is in honor of the beginning of the balneological technical school holiday. Today there will be a big outdoor festival, with competitions in swimming and archery and other such events. Now we must continue on up."

They went up along a steep stairway hewn out of the rock, and came out on Sea Treasures Street.

"Here is our house," said Mikhail, and he gestured toward a small cottage with a colored tile roof and a veranda entwined with grapevines.

Before he went through the garden gate, Platonov looked around. Far below, blended with the light blue sky on the horizon, lay the great ocean, deep-blue and beautiful.

And again he told himself that he had made no mistake in coming here.

He was pleased with his room. Cherry branches peeped through the open window, and the delicate scent of flowers poured in from the garden.

"Thank you, Mikhail," said Platonov, having placed his bags in the corner. "This chair is too good for me, too fragile. Don't you have another more ordinary one? You see, I'll have to do some work with chemical reagents."

"Very well, I'll give you another." Mikhail was silent,

expecting Platonov to say more about his work, but the old man said nothing. Then Mikhail suggested, "Let's go freshen up under the shower."

In the summer shower house, built in a corner of the garden, he looked with involuntary curiosity—the curiosity of a geriatrist, a specialist in old men—at Platonov's muscular body. No, this old fellow didn't look over forty at all. True, appearances can be deceiving. One would have to test his blood and check his heart.

Platonov snorted under the cool stream and beat his chest and shoulders with the palms of his hands. On his chest, old, long-healed, pink scars were visible beneath the reddish hair. And on his back, across his shoulder blades, stretched a wide scar with jagged edges. Mikhail suddenly remembered dimly: his mother had once told him that his Uncle Georgi had been a pilot during the war.

"In this town," said Platonov, "your boots probably wear out fast, eh?"

"Boots?" repeated Mikhail. "Yes, they wear out, of course. But why?"

Platonov didn't answer. He snorted a bit more and began drying himself briskly with a Turkish towel.

"That's a reminder of the fascists," he said, slapping on the chest. "Machine-gun fire. But *he* came out of it worse? Oh, how long ago that was—many years before you were born.... Do you have a family?"

"Yes. My son, as always, is down by the sea. But my wife will soon be back from work, and she'll give us supper. Perhaps you'd like to eat something meanwhile?"

"No, I'm not hungry. Let's talk first. Mikhail, my coming here must not change your household routine. I don't want to be in your way."

"You won't be in our way at all. On the contrary, I'm very glad that...."

"Now, now," Platonov raised his hand. "Emotion is a fluctuating thing; we won't speak of it."

They went from the shower house into the garden and headed toward the house.

The garden gate slammed; a quick patter of feet was heard. From behind the flower bed a blackened boy of about thirteen ran toward them.

"Papa!" he shouted, still at a distance. "I caught such a big mackerel!" He spread his hands wide and then fell silent in confusion, looking distrustfully at the stranger.

"Igor, meet your Uncle Georgi," said Mikhail.

"Hello, Igor," said Platonov seriously, without the usual adult condescension toward a child, and he shook the boy's slim hand. "Where did you leave your mackerel?"

"At Philip's. He'll clean it and fry it over the coals. Philip says he's never seen such a big mackerel. Are you going to live with us long?"

"Not very." Platonov tapped with his index finger on the boy's protruding collarbone. "Do you want to help me a little?"

"Yes," said Igor.

In the evening they ate supper on the veranda.

"May I offer you some more meat?" asked Asya, Mikhail Levitsky's wife. She avoided addressing him as Uncle Georgi. His youthful looks somehow aroused in her a hostile distrust.

"No thank you," said Platonov. "Both the meat and the vegetables are excellent. You're a good hostess, Asya."

The woman dryly thanked him and served her guest a cherry compote.

"Mama," said Igor, jiggling his feet, "tomorrow Uncle Georgi and I are going to the mouth of the Luza."

"That's nice. But why don't you simply go to Chalcedony Bay? The beach is better equipped there."

"Aw, old Chalcedonka! There's a million people under every tent."

"All the same it's better than dragging thirty kilometers in the heat to Luza."

"Well, if it's so far then we can just wander around the

neighborhood a little," said Platonov, sensing a certain displeasure in the woman's tone.

"No, no," cried Igor. "You said yourself that you wanted to take a long hike in these boots."

"What about the boots?" asked Asya.

Platonov looked at the woman's round face and pursed lips.

"I simply want to break in my new boots. Your stony roads are well suited for it."

"I was just thinking, don't you work in the shoe industry?"

"I've had some connection with that line. Would you be kind enough to give me some more compote?"

"Certainly," Asya served the compote from a pitcher. "And where do you work now?"

"At my specialty—biochemistry. I have to complete certain experiments, and then I plan to retire on a pension."

"You look well for a man of retirement age."

"Yes, many people say that," Platonov said calmly.

He ate the compote quietly, and then thanked his hostess and, pleading tiredness, went to his room. As he left, Asya followed him with a long stare.

"Igor," she said, "take the dishes into the kitchen. Wait! Why did Uncle Georgi send you to town?"

"He gave me a list of various things, and I ran to the radio store on the quay. Uncle Georgi is going to teach me to solder."

"That's good," said Mikhail. "Perhaps he'll give you a taste for technology. Otherwise you'll only know how to read books and fish with your Philip. Well, go on, don't break any dishes." And when the boy had seized the tray full of plates and glasses and dashed into the kitchen, Mikhail said quietly to his wife: "Asya, I want to ask you ... It seems to me that it isn't right to ask him any questions."

"Why is that?" Asya reacted with a start, so that the wicker chair squeaked under her plump body. "What kind of creature is he? You said he was over seventy and he looks your age."

"Well, Asya, that's no reason to treat him badly."

"All right. But I just don't like it when a man surrounds himself with secrecy."

"He's not surrounding himself with anything. You heard him—he needs to complete some kind of work."

"Well, I tell you, Mikhail, it would be better if he did his experiments somewhere else. Anything could happen— some equipment of his could explode or better than that, the house could burn down.... I'll ask at the resort adminis- tration for accommodations for him in a boarding house."

"No," said Mikhail firmly, and she looked at him in sur- prise. "No, Asya, he'll live with us as long as he wants to. He's my dead mother's brother. Except for us he has no rela- tives at all."

"As you wish." Asya got up and with a little brush she whisked the crumbs from the tablecloth onto a small tray. "As you wish, Misha. But I don't like it."

A rocket flew into the dark sky with a hiss, and spilled a handful of green and white lights straight into the Big Dip- per. Then a new rocket rose, and another, and another. Red spirals whirled in the sky and fell in a multicolored, starry rain.

Mikhail remembered that he had not watered the fruit trees that day. He went down to the garden and headed to- wards the tool shed for the garden hose. Rounding the cor- ner of the house, he stopped in the shadow of a cherry tree.

Platonov was standing in his darkened room opposite the open window. All at once a rocket lit up his head, which was turned toward the sky. Deep lines were sharply etched on his face, as though it were hewn out of stone. These lines ran from the tip of his nose to the corners of his hard mouth and deepened on his square chin. His face was peaceful, but Mikhail sensed in it a certain immeasureable tiredness. Such an expression may be seen on the faces of people who don't have anything more to look forward to in life.

Mikhail stepped back. The cockle shells crunched under his feet, and Platonov saw him and smiled.

"There's a big celebration going on in Kara-Buroon," he said.

"Yes," said Mikhail. "We always mark the balneological school holiday this way."

Platonov had already been living for two weeks in the home of his nephew. He would get up at dawn and awaken Igor, who slept in the garden on a folding cot. They would drink a glass of cold milk and go off into the hills. At that hour Mikhail and Asya were still asleep.

For the morning walk Platonov would wear his new brown boots with the yellow soles, and he gave the boy the same sort of boots, but a fairly well-worn pair. They were a little big for Igor, who wore three pairs of socks so that his feet wouldn't move about in them, and bore stoically the inconvenience of the heavy equipment.

After about three hours they would come back, painstakingly clean the road dust from their boots, and just as painstakingly weigh them on a sensitive scale. Then Platonov would put his boots in a special box, the bottom of which was lined with thick felt, soaked in some kind of solution. From this felt a wire led to an apparatus he had fitted up on the very first day of his arrival. After being weighed, Igor's boots were placed in an ordinary cardboard box.

Then the two friends—for they had indeed become friends, insofar as was possible with such an age difference—would eat a breakfast left by Asya, and work for a while. Platonov wrote and Igor solved problems set up by his uncle, or wound spools, or read something of his own. Sometimes Igor, chewing his pencil over a difficult problem, would glance at his uncle and notice that he was not writing, but sitting with his head in his hand. Not once did the boy think to disturb his meditations.

One day Ulatonov received two packages in the mail, sent from Leningrad by general delivery. He and Igor had to drag them up the stairway, for there were no taxis on Sea Treasures Street.

A day later still another heavy package arrived. Platonov threw his boots into a corner and no longer wore them during his morning walks, and Igor returned to his own comfortable sandals. Platonov's room was now crammed with instruments and entangled with wires; and needles, like grasses, stirred everywhere on dials. Platonov sat longer and longer over his work. Sometimes he would stop writing and say to Igor: "Go into the garden, little friend, and rest a bit. I must be alone."

Igor would climb into the hammock with his book and wait patiently. Usually around three o'clock, his uncle would come out onto the veranda, squint up at the sun and do several deep-knee bends. This meant that his working day was over and they could go down to the sea. But on one occasion he worked very late on something. Five o'clock went by and he still hadn't appeared on the veranda. Igor went quietly up to his uncle's door and listened. Not a sound came from the room. For some reason Igor started to feel uneasy, and he pushed the door open. . . .

Platonov lay prone on the floor. Igor cried out and hurriedly turned his uncle over on his back. Platonov opened his eyes which were glazed from unconsciousness.

"Undo me," he said hoarsely.

Igor tore tight rubber cuffs and wires from his uncle's wrists and ankles. His uncle slowly got up, then fell into a chair.

"What have you been doing to yourself?" Igor asked worriedly.

"Nothing. . . . Turn off the switch." He fell silent. His breathing became more even. "Well, that's it. Get your fishing rod an we'll go to the sea."

Not very far from the arch of Three Mile Way, among a conglomeration of shoreline rocks, there was a small triangular spot strewn with large pebbles. Igor had long ago chosen this place for swimming and fishing. Here he took Uncle

Georgi. They swam, then sat in the shade of a rock, facing the ocean; and Igor threw out his fishing line.

"How come you don't want to get a suntan?" asked Igor at one point, looking at Uncle Georgi's white skin.

"It wouldn't be very healthy for me," answered Platonov, "but you have enough tan for both of us."

Igor looked at his own brown stomach.

"My tan lasts the whole year. Philip says that if you get properly tempered by the sun, you won't catch any kind of disease. But you can't get burned because of your old wounds, is that it?"

"Partly. But the main reason is that I am very old."

"You're not old at all. You swim better than I do, especially the butterfly. Uncle Georgi, stay with us forever, all right?"

"All right, my friend. Reel in, you've got a bite."

On the way home they dropped in on Philip, who had converted a natural grotto in a big rock into a workshop, so skillfully that it seemed to belong to the city of Kara-Buroon.

The walls of the grotto were hung with photos cut from magazines. The selection was strictly limited—ships and girls. Philip himself had been a sailor, which explained his attachment to naval themes. As for the second part of the picture gallery, Philip said eloquently that it paid tribute "to the eternal and imperishable ideal of beauty."

The soles of one's shoes wore out quickly in Kara-Buroon, and old Philip had lots of work. He combined his work with fishing, fixing a line with bells attached to it under a rock. He knew people and footwear well. He could tell a man's character from the worn sole of his shoe. And he could talk without letting the nails drop from his mouth.

Sometimes Platonov would bring a bottle of red wine. Philip would grill a mackerel on the coals and they would have a feast. Tapping with his hammer, directing his knife on the cutting board, Philip told stories about people, ships and soles.

"Everything in this world goes to seed—both trees and

women," he proclaimed. "The sea alone is imperishable and eternal because no one can drink it up, not even all-powerful time."

And he looked at his companions triumphantly, as if to say: "Well now, what do you say to that?"

Platonov didn't reply, but Igor put in that if a billion years passed then the sea, too, might simply evaporate.

"That will never be," said Philip with conviction, and taking a nail from his mouth, he drove it into the sole. "You're a good boy, but you're psychologically unprepared." And with one blow of his hammer he pounded in the nail.

Sometimes Platonov and Igor made their way to Chalcedony Bay along an old forest road. But they didn't go all the way to the resort. From a distance Platonov would look at the white boarding houses, the gaily-colored tents, and the beaches swarming with people; then they would turn back.

They preferred another road to the bay, the one followed by the electric train. This road was cut into a mountain ridge. A gorge, intersected by the open-work girders of the railway bridge, cut across the rocky promontory, creating a steep precipice as it neared the sea. Farther along the edge of the precipice there was a narrow ledge. To walk on it was difficult, but from this great height one got a good view of the long yellow beaches of Chalcedony Bay.

One time they decided to walk along the narrow ledge. Igor walked ahead slowly, and Platonov moved after him step by step, with his hand outstretched, ready at a moment's notice to support the boy should he stumble.

"That's enough, Igor," he said at last. "It's completely impassible beyond this point. Stop."

They leaned back against the rough, sun-warmed cliff and looked for a long time at the sea lazily rocking below beneath the precipice.

"It's nice here," Platonov said quietly, as if to himself.

"Could you dive down from here?" asked the boy.

"I don't know. Let's just go back now."

They came out on Three Mile Way at the spot where

a monument stood over the common grave of the sailors who had defended Kara-Buroon during the war.

"Uncle Georgi, tell me about the war."

"I've told you a lot, my little friend. But if you want..."

And he, as he had so many times already, began to tell about the air and tank battles, about the submarines, and about the fascists, who could not be tolerated on this planet if people wanted to live happily.

And as they talked, they slowly climbed up the steps in the rock onto Sea Treasures Street.

"What is the date today?" asked Platonov, as he opened the garden gate.

"August seventeenth. Gee, that's too bad. I'll soon have to go back to school."

"The seventeenth already," repeated Platonov in a low voice, and went into the garden.

Asya had a curious nature. The secret surrounding Platonov gave her no peace. Of course she remembered her husband's advice not to bother their guest with questions, but she couldn't resist asking her son about Platonov. But Igor didn't give away any secrets, since he knew very little—indeed he knew nothing.

It was a quiet evening. The stars were spread out across the black sky, and through the trees you could see the silvery path of the moon on the sea.

Mikhail Levitsky sat on the veranda and read his newspaper, now and then commenting with an approving or an ironic "hm-m." Asya set the table and called Igor.

"What, Mom?" Igor said, as he appeared, a book in hand.

"What is Uncle Georgi doing?"

"He's working."

"He works too much. What is he endlessly writing about day and night, I'd like to know.... Call him to come and have tea."

"Tea, that's nice," he said, sitting down at his place. "An

eternal and imperishable beverage, as our friend Philip would say. What do they say in the paper, Mikhail?"

"Oh, the same as usual." Mikhail put aside the paper. "Deep well drilling continues on the Tsion Plateau. There's an international symposium of philosophers. They mention Professor Neuman's mysterious death again."

"Hand me the paper." Platonov ran through the account of the symposium. "You're right, it's just the usual thing.... Oh, strawberry jam, perfect! Well, Mikhail, how are your old folks coming along?"

"What's gotten into him," thought Mikhail, "nervous excitement or just good mood?"

He began to talk about the newest methods they were using to treat old age in the Longevity Sanatorium, and Platonov listened and asked questions which demonstrated a knowledge of the subject, while Asya kept giving him more strawberry jam.

"Yes," said Platonov pensively, "from Hippocrates to our own day people have struggled with the problem of longevity ... " He looked at Mikhail, narrowing his eyes. "Tell me, nephew, what in your opinion is the main cause of aging?"

"A complicated question, Uncle Georgi.... In general I agree with the view that old age is the gradual loss of the capacity of living matter for self-renewal. It's true the general development of life is linked with the inevitability of death, but something is needed to prepare.... " Mikhail tilted back in his chair; his voice took on the tone of a lecturer. "You undoubtedly know that the efficiency of metabolism in a nine-year-old child reaches fifty percent, while in an old man of ninety it goes down to thirty. The intake of oxygen and the release of carbon dioxide are altered; unstable proteins assume more stable forms and so on. I want to point out that in old age the organism adjusts to the changes of aging, and we geriatrists consider it our chief problem to stabilize this adjustment as long as possible."

"Right, Mikhail, but hasn't it occurred to you that the

organism.... Oh, never mind," Platonov interrupted himself. "All this is too boring for Asya."

"Oh, no, please. I'm used to such conversations," said Asya. "I've been wanting to ask you: Do you work in Leningrad?"

"Not far from there, in Borky. It's a Scientific Community."

"Well, of course," said Asya, "who doesn't know Borky? Last year we treated an important physicist from Borky. He was a wonderful fellow, gay and sociable. We all simply fell in love with him."

Platonov looked attentively at her and met an equally searching look from Asya.

"Asya," he said, smiling at his own thoughts, "Asya and Mikhail ... I realize, of course, that I have not been very polite. This old fellow comes out of nowhere and lives here for three weeks without saying more than three words about himself or his work ... No, no, Mikhail, be quiet. I know that it's so, even though I appreciate your tactfulness. Well, now perhaps it's time for me to explain a few things.... "

He was silent for a minute, then he wiped his brow with the plam of his hand and began:

"It came to me many years ago, during the third year of the war, to be more exact. It was before your time, and I was young and healthy as an ox. It all started from something nonsensical. But at the time it wasn't nonsense to me ... Do you remember Dickens, Mikhail? The King's Counsel* asks Sam Weller if anything particular had happened to him on the morning in question. And Sam says, 'Yes Sir, that morning, gentlemen of the Jury, I received a new suit, and that was a very particular and uncommon circumstance for me.' In the same way, one morning I got a new leather coat —a raglan they call it—and for me this was a particular event too. We young aviators loved to show ourselves off.

I attached shoulder pieces to the coat and sewed on tabs.

---

* Prosecuting attorney in an English court. [Tr.]

Then they called me out, and fifteen minutes later I was already in the air. Sporting my new coat, I came face to face in another fifteen minutes with a fascist and went into a head-on attack. I've told you this umpteen times, Igor, and you know that in such a situation everything depends on your nerve. Whoever gives up first veers off to one side and gets a burst of fire in an unprotected spot. Well, we got closer and closer and I got hit. But in the heat of the moment I felt nothing at first. I pressed forward toward him. It all happens in a matter of seconds, you know. He pulled away and up, exposing his belly to my fire, and I gave it to him in his oil tank. He was smoking; I remember seeing that. He started smoking and went down. How I landed that machine I don't know. The boys said the whole cabin was running with blood. In a word, it was a miracle that I survived. They dragged me out and got me to a hospital. Six holes right through the chest. Well anyway, I lay there, and gradually recovered, and was eventually discharged. . . . But my new raglan—to this day I get angry when I think of it . . . in front the holes were small, but in back it was a complete mess. I thought: 'how ridiculous, my own holes are all healed up, but on the raglan they're still gaping. . . . Do you get the idea, nephew?"

"Not yet," said Mikhail.

"It didn't come to me right away either. But I began to think. Of course with a war on, your mind is not on serious study, but still I began to read special books when I could. Then after the war I went into the reserves. I joined a chemistry faculty, and began to work in earnest. You see, on the one hand we have leather footwear, and leather soles wear out. But when a live man goes barefoot and wears down his skin, it grows back again. And I thought: Would it be possible to do something so that inaminate skin, the sole of a shoe, could restore itself?"

"A useless labor," smiled Mikhail. "Leather is almost never employed in soles now. Synthetics. . . . "

"Go on, you and your synthetics!" Platonov made a wry face. "What a character you are. I'm talking to you about a philosophical problem. Now just look at the phenomenon of wear and tear on a higher plane. All of its instances can be divided into two categories. The first is gradual wear and tear, a gradual change in quality. Shoes, for example—both leather and synthetic. As soon as you set foot in new shoes they begin to wear out. To determine exactly at what point they wear out is difficult. It depends on the individual. One person decides his shoes are worn out and throws them away. Another picks them up and thinks: 'Aha, someone has thrown out almost new boots; I'll try them for a while. . . . '"

Mikhail gave a short laugh.

"Now take another category: abrupt wearing out," Platonov continued. "An example is the electric light bulb. Here, I turn on the light. Can you say how many hours the light has been burning? When will it burn out?"

"Actually," said Mikhail, "the light doesn't wear out in the same sense. It burns and burns, and suddenly goes out."

"Exactly!" Platonov got up and walked around on the veranda, his hands thrust into his pockets. "It suddenly burns out. A single step, an instant changeover into a new state. . . . Of course the overwhelming majority of things are subject to the first, gradual type of wear. And I began to think: Would it be possible to condition shoe leather so that it fits into the second category—so that it wears out abruptly, rather than gradually? Let's assume that you wear shoes long and hard, but their soles always stay just like new. Then at the end of a long period of time, one fine day they fall apart in the twinkling of an eye, so that no one could possibly wear them any longer. Like an electric light bulb—Pop! and that's it. . . . "

Platonov suddenly fell silent. He leaned on the railing as though he were watching something in the darkness of the garden.

"It's an interesting thought," said Mikhail. "A thing is continually new until a fixed time."

"And did you make such shoes, ones that don't wear out?" asked Asya.

"Yes."

"But how did you do that?" asked Mikhail, becoming interested.

"It's a long story, my friend. In general, we have reached the point, after long years of experimentation, where leather from an organic source will restore its own worn cells. But you see, shoe leather isn't such an important problem. It's the principle behind it which has led me . . . and others . . . rather far. . . ." Platonov straightened up. "But more about this some other time."

"Will you have more tea?" said Asya. "I thought right away that you were an inventor. Does it mean that one could make a coat and other things and they would always be like new?"

"Yes, you can make a coat. . . . But I'll be going now. . . ."

"Are you going to work all night again?"

"Possibly."

At this point they heard a knocking at the garden gate. Igor ran to open it.

"Is this the Levitsky house?" a high female voice carried to the veranda.

"Yes," answered Igor.

"Tell me, please, does Georgi Platonov live with you?"

Platonov's eyebrows shot up when he heard this voice. Slowly he descended from the veranda and went to meet a slender young woman in a gray suit who was following Igor along the garden path.

"Georgi!"

She flung herself upon him and buried her face in his chest. He took hold of her trembling shoulders; his eyes were half closed.

"Why did you come?" he said. "How did you find me?"

The woman raised her face, wet with tears.

"I found you, that's all. . . ."

"Come to my room. We'll talk."

He took her by the hand and led her to his room, murmuring an apology on the way.

"It's all right," Asya called out. Pursing her lips, she looked at her husband. "Well! What do you say to that?"

"What a face she has," said Mikhail quietly.

"I wish she had said hello to us. . . . Anyway, your old uncle has rather young friends, don't you think?"

"Maybe she's his wife. . . . "

"His wife? Then you think he ran away from his wife? A nice guy he is!"

"Stop it, Asya. Can't you see, something happened between them."

"I see, I see. I see everything." Asya began to rinse out the glasses.

Mikhail went down into the garden, got the hose out of the shed, and fitted it to the water spout. He tried not to look in at Platonov's window, but he could see out of the corner of his eye that the light was out.

A thin stream played from the hose. The ground, the grass, and the trees drank thirstily, and Mikhail didn't spare the water, so that they might get all they needed.

Then he returned to the veranda and sat down again; and Asya said: "We must go to bed."

Mikhail didn't answer.

"What is it, Misha? Do you hear me?"

"Yes. I don't feel like sleeping."

She went up to him from behind and put her plump arms around his neck.

"I wish he would leave soon, Misha. Don't be angry, but it seems to me. . . . He brings some kind of discord into our life. . . . It was so peaceful when we didn't know him. . . ."

He stroked her arm.

They heard footsteps. Asya walked away toward the veranda railing and stood, her arms crossed. What else was going to intrude upon them?

The glass door opened quietly. Platonov and the woman in the gray suit came out onto the veranda.

"I must apologize to you," said the woman. On her pretty face she wore the embarrassed smile of a child who knows he is forgiven. "I am Galina Kulomzina. I was Georgi Ilich's assistant in Borky for some time."

Mikhail hurriedly moved a wicker chair toward her.

"Please sit down."

"Thank you. I'm used to looking after Georgi, and ... in short, I came here on the *Balaklava* and have walked all over town. You have such a beautiful town, only the flights of steps are very tiring...."

"That's true." Mikhail smiled. "You have to get used to Kara-Buroon."

"I didn't know where Georgi was staying, and I asked literally everyone I met, giving a description of him. A silly, hopeless procedure, don't you think...? I even went to Chalcedony Bay and went around to all the boarding houses. At last it occurred to me to go to the resort administration. Fortunately one woman employed there knew that one of her fellow workers... you"—she smiled at Asya—"had a relative visiting her...."

"Ah," said Asya, "all's well that ends well."

"Yes.... I'm dreadfully tired, but, thank God, I've found him." Galina stared at Platonov, who stood motionless at the railing.

"May I get you some tea?" asked Asya.

"In a minute, Asya," Platonov broke in. "First, would it be possible for Galina to find a room here with a neighbor?"

Asya looked at him in surprise.

"It's already rather late," she spoke hesitantly. "But.... Why not with us... can't your assistant stay with us? Igor sleeps in the garden, his room is free."

"Of course," said Mikhail. "Make yourself comfortable in Igor's room."

"Thank you," Galina sighed. "I'm so tired. . . ."

"By the way, where did Igor go?" said Asya, and she looked into the garden. "Igor!"

After the strange woman had flung herself at Uncle Georgi, Igor had quietly withdrawn into the shadow of the trees. He made his way into a far corner of the garden and sat down on the edge of a rock. A disturbing feeling of an imminent parting overtook him. And Igor decided he would never get married for any reason, because wherever a woman appears, right away everything turns topsy-turvy.

The next morning Platonov disappeared.

Igor discovered it first. For three weeks he had been used to Uncle Georgi waking him before dawn, but this morning he woke up by himself. Igor could tell by the sun that his usual hour of waking up was long past. Feeling that some kind of unpleasant change was in the air, he went into the house, stepping quietly in his bare feet, and opened the door to Platonov's room a crack.

His uncle wasn't there. His equipment was all piled in one corner in disarray.

Clearly, he had gone up into the hills alone.

No one had ever offended Igor more bitterly. In order not to cry, the boy quickly climbed into a nut tree, the tallest one in the garden, and began to look down at the sea, pale blue and silvery at this early hour. A white motor ship was sailing out of the bay and turning slowly to the right.

"The *Balaklava*," thought Igor. And he imagined to himself how one fine day he would sail away on the white motor ship out of Kara-Buroon and then arrive in Borky and live with Uncle Georgi and help him with his work. He kept looking at the road to see whether Uncle Georgi was coming back, and he imagined beforehand how he would answer his uncle's greetings dryly and make it a little bit difficult for him before accepting any suggestion to go down to the sea together.

Then the woman from yesterday came out onto the veranda. She wore a lightweight sarafan—blue and white. She looked anxiously to either side and went back into the house. Next his father appeared on the veranda. He, too, looked around, straightened the grapevine, and called out, "Igor!"

Igor reluctantly answered.

"Come on, climb down quickly," said his father. "Have

you seen Uncle Georgi this morning? No? Where has he gone?"

His father's voice sounded unusual, and Igor understood: something had happened.

They were all standing in Uncle Georgi's room. Mikhail turned over in his hands a big sealed packet, on which was written: "To Mikhail Levitsky. Do not open this until the morning of August 24th." That meant tomorrow morning. . . .

Platonov's things were not in the room; he had taken both suitcases with him. Only his instruments remained and his empty shoe box, and two or three books.

"What's he done, gone off without saying good-by?" asked Asya shaking her head. "Without saying one word. . . . "

Galina looked at the package in Levitsky's hands. Her anxious eyes were fixed unblinkingly upon it.

"He's gone?" Igor asked in confusion.

And then he remembered about the *Balaklava* sailing out of town, and told the others.

"Now we'll find out," said Mikhail and, not letting the packet out of his hands, he went to the telephone.

He called the dispatcher at the marine station, who agreed to contact the *Balaklava* by radio.

"Mikhail Petrovich," said Galina in a high jangling voice, "I beg of you, open the packet."

"No, Galina," he answered, "that I cannot do."

"It's a strange thing," murmured Asya, "to quit such comfortable lodgings at his age. . . . "

Galina looked at her.

"Excuse me for my inappropriate curiosity. . . . You simply can't imagine how important this is. . . . Do you know how old Georgi. . . . Georgi Ilich is?"

"I can answer you," said Mikhail. "Uncle Georgi was twenty years older than his sister, my late mother. He's seventy-three or seventy-four years old."

"Seventy. . . . My God. . . !" whispered Galina, pressing her hands to her cheeks.

Now it was Asya's turn to marvel.

"You worked with him and you didn't know how old he was?"

"He never told me. . . . I didn't work with him long—four years. . . . But the old-timers said that he looked almost the same as he had many years before. I only knew he was older than Neuman. . . ."

"Uncle Georgi worked with Neuman?" said Mikhail in disbelief.

"Yes."

"But wait a minute. . . . I'm well acquainted with Professor Neuman's work. He was concerned with the problem of longevity, and this is most interesting to me as a geriatrist. But Uncle Georgi worked in a completely different area. He talked about wear on materials—something about the conversion of gradual wear into the sudden wear category. What do they have in common?"

"I can't explain now. . . . I'm not in a position to talk about this. . . . " Galina looked pale. "But it was precisely with sudden wearing out in mind that they began their crazy experiment. . . . " She turned toward the window.

"What did happen to Neuman?" asked Asya with interest. "They said in the papers that it was a mysterious, sudden death, that he hadn't been at all sick. . . . My dear, what is wrong?" she cried, seeing that Galina was weeping. "Oh, please, calm yourself. Igor, get some water quickly!"

"There's no need." Galina sobbed. "It's just that I have the most distressing fears. . . . Mikhail Petrovich, open the packet!"

Mikhail slowly shook his head.

Then the telephone rang, and he grabbed the receiver quickly.

"Doctor Levitsky?" he heard. It was the dispatcher from the marine station. "I contacted the *Balaklava* by UKV. Georgi Platonov does not appear on the passenger list."

"Thank you," said Mikhail, and hung up. "He's not on the *Balaklava*."

"That means he's here!" shouted Igor.

"Yes, you can only leave Kara-Buroon by sea," Asya confirmed. "Dear, there's no need to worry. . . ."

"I'll go." Galina started for the door. "I'll go to search for him."

"I'll go with you!" Igor jumped up.

"Just a minute." Mikhail stood in their way; his dry, thin-lipped face looked very worried, very serious. "Listen to me a minute, Galina. You must figure this out logically. Georgi left with his suitcases, and they're rather heavy. Naturally he wouldn't go wandering all over town with such a load. As soon as he could, he must have stopped at a hotel or put his suitcases in the checkroom at the station. I can inquire much more quickly by phone than you can by roaming around the town. I beg you, be patient. There are only three hotels in the whole town.

Galina nodded, and went to the window.

"Igor, you must go and wash," Mikhail said in a low voice, and picked up the receiver again.

He rang the Hotel Southern and the other two hotels, and they all answered that Georgi Platonov wasn't there and hadn't stopped by.

Mikhail glanced at his watch, called the Longevity Sanatorium, and asked the head doctor's permission to be an hour late. Then came a complicated conversation with the administration of the marine station, the upshot of which was that they found out for sure that no one by the name of Georgi Platonov had left two big suitcases in the checkroom that morning.

All this time Galina sat motionless by the window, and Igor, not thinking of going off to wash, mechanically turned the pages of a book that Uncle Georgi had left behind.

"He must be staying at Chalcedony Bay," said Mikhail, calling the switchboard of the resort.

"Quiet!" Galina cried suddenly. "Someone is in the garden. . . ." She leaned out of the window.

Yes, it was the crunch of cockle shells underfoot. . . .

Galina ran onto the veranda, and everyone followed her.

Along the garden path toward the veranda came a heavy man in white netting and coarse linen trousers, with sandals on his bare feet. The sweat had pasted a strand of gray hair to his brow. Huge drops ran down his dark, bronzed face.

"Philip!" Igor ran to meet the old shoemaker.

"Hello, boy," said Philip, catching his breath. "Hello, everyone."

He came up onto the veranda and sat down in a chair. Four pairs of anxious eyes stared at the old man.

"There was a time when a steep climb aroused in me a desire to sing," said Philip, breathing noisily and quickly.

"Have you seen Uncle Georgi?" Igor asked impatiently. "Where is he?"

"I was digging under a rock for worms to sell, and the sun had not yet risen," said Philip, and he scratched his shaggy gray eyebrow with his little finger. "Then he came along. He had a suitcase in each hand and a blade of grass in his teeth. 'Philip, I'm planning to leave. May I leave my suitcases with you for a while?' Well, if there are no atomic bombs in them, you can—in that way I let him know he could put them in the corner. We sat and had a breakfast of tomatoes and cheese. He ate little and talked even less." Philip paused, and gazed with a long, approving look at Galina. " 'How old are you,' he asked me, and I said, 'a man doesn't need to know how old he is, because. . . .' "

"Where is he?" Galina interrupted. "If you know, then simply tell us. Where is he?"

Philip shook his head.

"That's too simple, my beauty," he said. "But I'll tell you all I know. The man who interests you so much pulled a pair of boots out of his suitcase and gave them to me, They don't wear out, he said, and that is the best thing I can give you, a specialist. I took the boots and, inasmuch as I don't believe in the eternal life of shoe leather. . . ."

"My God, really, is it humanly possible for you to tell us where he is?"

"Humanly? Aha, humanly. . . . Well, he shook hands with me in farewell and went up long Three Mile Way. He was going for a walk—that's what he said. I started to work and thought it over: 'What kind of look was that on his face?' It had struck me as strange. And I decided to come here and tell you what you have heard. Humanly. . ! Bring me some water, sonny."

"Mama will bring it!" Igor was running from the veranda. "I know where to look for him!" The boy's voice was already coming from behind the trees. "I'll find him!"

The gate slammed.

Philip drank the water, looked at Galina, nodded and started for the gate. The shells crunched under his heavy tread. Mikhail went to see him off.

"Doctor, I've been wanting to ask you," said Philip, taking hold of the latch, "give me something so that I won't sweat so much in my sleep."

Igor ran over the uneven flagstones of Three Mile Way. The stiff grass sticking up through the cracks scratched his bare feet. He had darted out of the house wearing only a pair of shorts, without any kind of hat, and now the sun was beginning to scorch his head.

He hurried.

The road became steeper. Igor was out of breath, and he slowed from a run to a quick walk. He tried to control his breathing regularly and economically, the way Uncle Georgi had taught him. Four steps—inhale; four steps—exhale.

Igor didn't know himself why he was in such a hurry. Up to now he had lived in a world of ordinary everyday objects and events. But these last events—the arrival of a strange woman, the mysterious flight of Uncle Georgi, Philip's visit—all this had bewildered the boy. He wanted one thing only: to cling to Uncle Georgi's strong hand; then everything would be all right again.

Three Mile Way ended. To the left the forest road led toward Chalcedony Bay, but Igor knew that his uncle didn't like this road: he always preferred to stick closer to the sea. And Igor unhesitatingly turned to the right, taking the narrow path that zigzagged down toward the ravine. At first he walked in the shadow of the railroad bridge. He pushed right through a wild pomegranate bush and then, picking his way through a grove of nut trees, he climbed the opposite wall of the ravine and approached the steep precipice above the sea.

He rested for a minute and rubbed his big toe, which had been painfully bruised on the root of a tree.

Then Igor moved on along the narrow ledge, where he and Uncle Georgi had once been. He tried not to look down at the sea shining deep blue below the precipice. He moved slowly, keeping his left shoulder in contact with the cliff and stepping cautiously over the brambles which lay here and there along the ledge. At one spot he noticed a trampled bush with crushed berries, which convinced him that Uncle Georgi had come that way not long before.

"Yes, he's not far away. Probably beyond that bend where a view of Chalcedony beach suddenly opens up. Still ten meters to go. . . ."

A wild rumbling and wailing broke in so suddenly upon Igor's thoughts that he started. Right above the boy's head an electric train flew over the steel bridge across the ravine and along the line cut in the rocks above the ledge. Igor knew that he couldn't see the train from there, but involuntarily he threw back his head, and instantly his right foot went over the edge.

He fell. . . .

His hand clutched desperately at the ledge, but it slipped off the smooth, rounded stone. Then Igor felt his stomach scrape against a thorny bush. He managed to clasp his hands to the bush, and hung over the precipice, vainly trying to gain a foothold.

"Uncle Georgi-i-i!"

"I-i-i. . . ." answered an ethereal echo.

Not long before, Georgi Platonov had moved along the ledge to the spot around the bend from where Chalcedony Bay could be seen.

He stopped, leaned back against the warm cliff, and pushed his cap back.

Here no one could see him and he didn't have to think about the expression on his face.

He was alone with his private thoughts.

Before him lay the vast ocean, warmed by the southern sun. He could see the green slopes of the mountains, the yellow beaches and white buildings. Two hours' walk away a beautiful woman was waiting for him. . . .

But he was already far, infinitely far from all that.

He knew that it was useless to put off what he must do any longer, but he simply couldn't stop thinking of Galina. . . .

"You understand, I had to run away from you! You disturbed me. I needed some kind of mental equilibrium in order to finish my work. But you were a disturbing influence, and so I left in secret—ran away from you. It was better that way—better for both of us. You would have understood everything from my notes that Mikhail was to send to Borky. And time would have healed the wounds."

"But you looked for me. . . . You looked for me."

"How can I explain to you, my dear one, that already I no longer belong to life? Yes, I am healthy and strong in spite of my seventy-four years. My movements are precise, my muscles are strong, and my heartbeat is steady. But in a few hours. . . . In just ten hours and twenty minutes. . . ."

"That poor devil Neuman: things were easier for him— after all, he didn't know ahead of time."

"The law of the conservation of metabolism that I have discovered is inevitable in its action. Nothing can save me. Nothing and no one, not even you. All the same, the crazy experiment I have completed here *might* make it possible. . . . No, not for me. For others, who will come after me. . . . Perhaps, following my directions, they will be able to overcome the law of the conservation of metabolism. . . . And that will mean that my work here, in silence and peace, has not been in vain."

"In silence and peace?"

There was no need to deceive himself. There had been no peace.

"But I didn't know I would meet this boy here."

"And if I had known. . . ?"

He had delayed long enough. Platonov looked at his watch. The second hand circled quickly, punctually counting off the time.

He would have to make up his mind now.

The electric train rumbled over his head. It was carrying gay, welldressed men and women to the velvety beaches.

"Well, Georgi Platonov, can you finally tear yourself loose from this warm rock?"

"Uncle Georgi-i-i!"

Igor? How had he gotten here?

The boy's voice, calling for help, at once brought Platonov back to life. He moved swiftly along the ledge, skirting sideways around its outcroppings. He eyes opened wide when he caught sight of the boy hanging over the precipice.

"Hold on, Igor! I'm coming!"

But the roots of the bush Igor was clinging to suddenly gave way. Still clutching the thorny branches, he fell through the air.

"A-a-a-a. . . ." His voice died away.

In that very instant Platonov pushed himself off the ledge and flung his body into the air. The dark blue sea rushed up toward him. Holding his outstretched hands together in front of his head, he cut like a knife, without a splash, into the water.

"This is going to hurt a little."

The boy nodded. The whole time his father was bathing his skinned chest and stomach, smearing him with ointment and bandaging him up, Igor didn't make a single sound. He lay with his teeth clenched, holding Uncle Georgi's hand tightly with his left hand. He didn't cry out and didn't moan. The pain and the crying were expressed only in his eyes.

"Well, that's all." Mikhail covered his son with a sheet. "You're a brave lad, Igor. Now try to go to sleep."

He laid his hand on the boy's brow, then he walked away from the bed and made a sign to his wife: "Let's leave, he needs rest." Asya got up with a sigh.

"Does that feel better, my little son?"

"Yes, Mama," whispered Igor.

He still kept holding the hand of Uncle Georgi, who was sitting motionless next to his bed. Asya drew the blinds and followed Mikhail out of the room.

Platonov lifted his head, his glance fell upon Galina. He smiled wearily at her and thought: "she's looking at me almost with hostility."

After a while Igor fell asleep. But as soon as Platonov tried gently to free his hand, the boy roused himself and squeezed Uncle Georgi's fingers still harder.

This happened several times.

Time passed. The room began to darken. Outside the window, the sun was setting. Platonov glanced furtively at his watch. Galina sat opposite, facing him, and in response to her desperate look he nodded his head silently.

At last he was able to pull his now numbed hand free. Igor was breathing evenly in his sleep. Platonov put his arm around Galina's shoulders and they went out onto the veranda.

Asya began to bustle about. She ran into the kitchen and returned with a tray. Platonov felt light-headed at the smell of food.

"Don't bother, Asya," he said. "I really couldn't eat any supper. Just relax. . . . What do they say in the papers, Mikhail?"

"I don't know," Levitsky answered, raising his eyebrows. "I haven't read anything today."

An evening breeze rustled through the leaves of the trees. Below, from the town, came the song of violins and the dry sound of a drum.

Platonov straightened up, and the wicker chair squeaked.

"Well, why are you staring at me?" he asked, almost roughly. "What's there to be excited about, an old man who has lived out his time on this earth. . . ."

No one answered him. After a while, Asya said timidly: "Georgi Ilich, you must be hungry. . . ."

"If you wish, give me some compote."

He began to eat the compote.

Galina suddenly got up.

"Georgi. . . ."

"Sit down, Galya," he interrupted her. "I beg you, sit down," he repeated softly. "I know that I have to tell you now. . . . I wanted to go before my time, but Igor got in my way. . . . Listen, Mikhail, you know old men well—you know these terrible changes that come with aging, the diseases of senility, weakness. . . . The gradual inevitable wearing out of the organism. . . . A man growing decrepit—damn it, what could be sadder?" A stubborn spark, familiar to Galina, began to glow in his gray eyes. "My fussing with leather and other materials led me to think about transforming the wear on a living organism into the sudden wear category. A man doesn't have to wear out gradually, like a shoe. When he has reached full physical maturity, let him stay in that condition—until the very end. Until his very last breath!"

Platonov got up and walked around the veranda. Then he sank into his chair again and continued more calmly.

"I struggled for many years and racked my brains. Then I started to work with Neuman. We decided that in order to stabilize an organism in its mature phase it would be necessary to relieve the electrical tension on several groups of brain cells. So that they would lose none of their bio-electrical energy, but receive some energy from without, in the form of periodic charges. . . . But, you will find it all in my notes —the theoretical premises and descriptions of our proceedures. I had to repeat the original experiments with the boots. Of course it was good for my mental equilibrium. . . . Then I received my instruments and. . . . Well, in short, I hurried so as to complete my work before August twenty-third—and I have succeeded, as you can see. . . . Mikhail, give my packet to Galina, she will take it to Borky."

"This means that you. . . ." Mikhail began in a hollow voice.

"Yes. We had no other choice but to experiment on ourselves. And we did that—Neuman and I. It was a very powerful dose—we took it all at once. You remember, Galya, last year we repeated. . . ."

"I remember!" she cried. "Yes. . . . If I had known what you were planning, I would have smashed the magnetic modulator!"

She began to sob. Asya silently stroked Galya's shoulders.

"Horrible. . . ." whispered Mikhail.

"Horrible? No, my dear nephew, it's beautiful!" said Platonov forcefully. "Am I like *your* old men? No, sir! I'm over seventy and I'm still healthy and strong. It's horrible the other way. . . . I succeeded in formulating one problem for the computer. . . . Well, I was absolutely astounded when it deduced the law of the conservation of metabolism and reported the duration of the effect, accurate to the minute. . . . I said nothing to Neuman—his hour turned out to be nearer than mine. . . . Yes, Neuman was a happy man. He didn't know."

Platonov suddenly started toward the door and threw it open. Behind the door, in the hallway, stood Igor—his bandages white against his brown body. He clutched a book in his hand.

"Were you eavesdropping?" Platonov asked quietly.

The boy looked at him with anxious eyes. As if someone had pushed him from behind, he threw himself at Platonov and clung to him convulsively.

"Don't go away . . !" he cried. "Uncle Georgi, don't go away! Don't go away!"

Platonov stroked his head.

"Now, now, Igor, where did you get such an idea . . ? Calm down now. Be a man. I'm not going anywhere. . . ."

He led the boy to his room and ordered him into bed.

"Have you been awake long?"

"No," whispered Igor, "not long. . . . I turned on the light. I wanted to read, and then. . . ."

"It's all right. Now sleep, my little friend. Give me the book. What is it?"

"It's yours. You left it behind. . . . It's *The Portrait of Dorian Grey.*"

"So it is! Well, Igor, good night!"

"Good night, Uncle Georgi."

Platonov returned to the veranda. Pensively he leafed through the tattered pages of the book. Then he took out a fountain pen and wrote in a bold hand on the title page: "To the future scientist Igor Levitsky, in memory of that violator of the laws of nature, Georgi Platonov. Do not fear what is written here."

He laid the book on the table and glanced at his watch. "It's time. . . ."

He pressed Mikhail's trembling hand. Weeping, Asya threw her arms around his neck.

"We never . . . never. . . ." Mikhail tried to say something, but his tongue wouldn't obey him.

"Anyway, it's good we have seen each other," said Platonov. "Good and bad. . . . Now we must say farewell. Galina, please come and see me off."

They sat on a rock, still warm from the day which had just ended. The sea washed gently against the tiny rock-strewn beach. To the right the city lights were visible—the illumined cube of the marine station, a chain of lights along the waterfront.

"Igor and I often bathed here."

Galina didn't answer. It was as if she had turned to stone.

Platonov pulled her closer to him.

"Be sensible, Galina. . . . Go on with your work, do you hear? We must fight old age, only not to the extent that it's against the course of nature. Are you listening to me?

Sudden wearing out—it's a sound idea. But a man doesn't have to know his own hour of dying. It interferes with his life. . . . Go to Leningrad, go to Zybin. Give him the records of my last experiment. It points the way for future research. . . . Galya, pull yourself together. . . . Listen! I've discovered a method of overcoming the law of the conservation of metabolism. You and Zybin must carry my work to a practical conclusion."

He got up, took off his watch, looked at it one more time and dashed it against a rock. Then he flung it into the sea.

"I'm going, Galya. . . . Life came from the ocean. We carry the ocean in our salty blood. I want this to happen in the sea. . . ."

"I won't let you!" cried Galina, gripping his hands with all her strength. "I won't let you, I won't let you!" she repeated in a frenzy.

He stroked her head and shoulders. His face was turned toward the starry heavens, but he didn't see the stars: his eyes were tightly closed.

Then he firmly removed her hands, quickly stripped off his clothes, and walked into the warm black water. The pebbles crunched.

Sobbing, she rushed after him.

"Be a good girl, Galina. I have little time left, and I want to swim to the mouth of the bay. . . ."

For a while, as she stood on the shore, she could still see his head and arms at regular intervals as they appeared and disappeared. Then the darkness hid him, but for a long time Galina heard the soft splashing of water beneath his hands as he swam away into the night.

Translated by JUDITH M. CLIFFORD.

Robot Humor

B. ZUBKOV AND E. MUSLIN

To Each His Own

"First work, then pleasure," said the Computer, when it had finished solving a batch of first-degree equations, as it began gleefully to count up the commas in the 6th, 8th and 15th editions of the *Encyclopedia Britannica.*"

"Out of the Mouths of Babes. . . !"

"Our teacher told us that mankind evolved from a monkey."

"Nonsense! The computers dreamed that up just because they were jealous!"

"Well, if you're right, our teacher must be a computer, too!"

The Real Give-Away

"When the oceanographic expedition returned from the Pacific, I knew right away which crew members were the real scientists and which were robots."

"How?"

"Only the scientists had a suntan!"

"Tell it Like it Is!"

"To find the solution to this problem you've got to rack your brain," he said to his machine.

"I already did. Only my semiconductors are left!"

The Law of Conserving Energy

"Our firm *Thought* sells only the very latest and most unusual computers. Take this model, for example! This brand-new calculator will handle at least one-half your mental work."

"Only half! Well, in that case, I'll buy two of them!"

Nothing New Under the Sun

"How did you like the original waltz the musical computer has just composed?"

"I've always liked it. In fact, I've been crazy about it since way back."

Robot Chit-Chat

"You know, recently everyone's been taking me for a human!"

"And what's so surpising about that? You behave illogically enough!"

Questions, Questions!

"Daddy, what's a wood goblin?"

"Hm, how can I explain."

"Is it some sort of a person?"

"No, not exactly."

"Then it must be a robot. Does it live in the woods?"

"Yes, it lives in the woods."

"Then where does it get its electricity from?"

Barankin Wants to be a Robot

From a composition by a fourth-grade student on "What Will You Be When You Grow Up?"

"When I grow up, I'll be a robot. Everyone loves robots. When I fell off the fence and got a bump on my forehead, I got scolded and was locked in my room. But when our two robots unscrewed each other's heads, no one said a thing to them. It's so nice being a robot!"

Ingenious Lovers

Announcement: The Marriage Bureau of the New-Moon
District wishes to inform all citizens that there will be a ten-
day waiting period between the formal announcement of an
engagement and the wedding ceremony. Bride and groom are
strictly forbidden to use a time machine!"

"Not What Meets the Eye!"

"What a terrific speaker! He certainly proved that machines simply can't do genuine creative work!"

"Why, didn't you know that was old man Puxtolivansky
in person. The best robots in the business are at work on
his philosophical studies!"

"Things are Bad All Over!"

"To the Board of Directors of apartment complex Ultra-
Berry Tree: We request you to remove the workshop for
repairing time machines from the first floor of Building No.
7421. The shop has given us residents no end of trouble.
Time and again we find ourselves with seven Fridays in a
single week and with no two years being the same length.
On the second floor our children keep growing not by the
day but by the hour! Worst of all, though, throughout the
building monthly magazines are flowing in a steady stream
now!

Signed: Residents of Building 7412.

Date: February 42, God only knows what year!"

Easy Come, Easy Go

"You know, yesterday my new deluxe-model computer,
"Friend-188," developed a brilliant new Theory of Relativity!"

"Say that's a fantastic achievement!"

"Truly stupendous! But today it just as brilliantly dis-
proved the same theory."

It's the Big Things in Life . . ."

"Have you heard about the latest achievement of our design office? It's a quantitative meteorological forecaster. It predicts in detail what the weather will be on any date you name in 200 or even 500 years!"

"That's really something! Now how about asking it what tomorrow's weather will be like?"

"Tomorrow's weather! We don't deal in trivia."

A Super Skeptic

"Oh, horrors! Computer F-33 has just committed suicide."
"How come?"
"It lost its faith in cybernetics!"

Translated by NATASHA GREEN.

The Minotaur

GENNADY GOR

1

WHO IS HE? A book PEDLAR, or someone who was sent from
the unknown? He appeared in a local train car as if from
nowhere and vanished as though into nowhere, carrying a
bundle of out-of-date books and magazines.

Sometimes he also sold lottery tickets, turning the lever
of a round glass container, that narrow haven of chance,
shuffling fortune—so tantalizingly close and yet so unattain-
able. He reminded me of some great writer of the past, one of
those who stare at you from another century in a daguerreo-
type or in an oil portrait. Bret Harte, Stevenson? No, perhaps
Dickens, after all. That's who he reminded me of.

Lithe and slender, resembling a hero and at the same
time a creator of old-fashioned books, everything in his appearance bespoke self-respect. He did not give his name, nor
the titles of his intellectual wares, but merely proffered them
silently. Yet, each time I looked at his thin, old-fashioned face,
I would become aware of an expression on it of slight astonishment and an expectation of something impossible, something at odds with all the laws of ordinary life.

And one day it happened. He came up to me in a
railway car and said quietly and politely in an extremely
pleasant voice, "Wouldn't you like to purchase a lottery
ticket?"

"No, I wouldn't," I answered. "I never win."

150

"What might you like to win?" he asked, looking at me with keen interest and concern.

"I always want the impossible, things one mustn't wish for. For example, I would wish to be given back my childhood, if only for an hour."

Why did I say that? It was an involuntary, tactless joke, and I regretted it. But he inquired with the same calm concern, "How do you know what is possible or impossible for me?"

Of course, I took his words as a joking remark, a display of original humor, but he continued:

"I will try to help you. Sometimes it works. With your permission, I'll call on you soon."

"But you don't even know my name, or my telephone number."

"Thank you," he said, and looked at me intently. "Now I know."

He smiled the way they must have smiled in the days of daguerreotypes. He bridged two centuries with his smile and left. Left? No, he seemed to have vanished into nowhere, as if beyond the doors of the train was the constellation of Lyra instead of the railway station.

Two or three weeks went by, and I had almost forgotten about that strange conversation, when the telephone on my desk rang and a pleasant, polite voice said, "Forgive me for bothering you. This is Dickens speaking."

"Which Dickens?"

"We met on the train."

"But you are not Dickens?"

"I look like him."

"Are you related, or do you just happen to look like him?"

"Neither, but there's no time to explain right now."

"Isn't it sort of awkward? He's a great classical writer, after all."

"Don't let that worry you."

"But who are you, really?"

"Faust, if you prefer."

"You sing in Gounod's opera?"

"Not quite. I sell books and lottery tickers, and in my spare time I try to link two worlds, mine and yours."

"To link two worlds? Is this some kind of a joke?"

"We don't have time for jokes. Do you really want to see your childhood?"

"I do."

"Then turn on the television right away."

2

Within a few moments I was watching on the screen the whole range of my childhood stretched out under my window, looking like a big, tired beast. And I saw myself among those whom time had borne away: grandfather, grandmother, and mother, acting out their lives right there, no more than two steps away from me, yet remaining in the irretrievable past.

Then, a few moments later only a little boy was left on the screen—a ten-year-old school boy who was myself almost fifty years ago. He was addressing me from the screen: "Why are you looking at me through the window? Come here. Join us."

"I'm only a spectator. I'm looking at a television screen, not a window."

"What's your name?" asked the little boy. I told him.

"They call me by that name. Are we namesakes?"

"No," I answered. "We are one and the same person. I am you—fifty years later."

The gentle, homely little boy, looking as though he had just stepped out of a snapshot in an old family album, smiled skeptically. "How do you know that I'll be like you in fifty years? Nobody knows about such things."

"I *am* you, understand? You, only after many, many years."

"But I don't want to be like you. I'd rather be a boy forever."

"You can't do that," I said. "Time is carrying you forward."

"Then please explain to me, am I in the future, or are you in the past?"

That was precisely what I could not explain to him, or even to myself. I began telling him about television, speaking slowly and logically, haunted all the while by the strange madness of the encounter.

"Now I see," said the boy. "I like an invention that makes it possible to meet yourself. But you only think you're me. Why don't you try and come in here, so we can really get acquainted."

He said that softly, almost inaudibly. And then the image disappeared, replaced by a news commentator. I heard the words: "The predatory policies of the neocolonial powers has led to . . . ." I was very glad to hear those words, that confident voice, that hackneyed phrase. Why? When we wake up, thus interrupting a dream, we are glad not only to return to the familiar world, but also to regain contact with ourselves. But, what I saw was too distinct and too real to have been a dream. My thoughts were suddenly interrupted by the telephone.

The familiar pleasant voice said, "Dickens speaking. How did you like the program?"

"What program?"

"The childhood."

"What childhood?"

"Your childhood."

"But that's impossible!"

"Don't you trust your own senses?"

"If you can perform such miracles, then why do you bother with selling books and out-of-date magazines?"

"Selling books is a serious, important trade."

"And miracles?"

"Just a joke, a game. One day you suddenly indulge your-

self and later you're sorry about it. I don't fool around with
that very often. Any old sorcerer or magician could also . . . ."
He paused.

"What do you mean, 'also?' You're neither a sorcerer nor
a magician. You're a book pedlar."

"That's true, I'm not a sorcerer, only a book pedlar. But
I must hang up now, I'm calling from a booth, and there's
already a line waiting. So long."

I'm not the sort of person who likes to kill time by
watching television. But now I saw my television set not
merely as a diversion, but as a window through which you
could see not only yourself, but even your past. I believed my
eyes more than the listings, which often announced the
dramatization of a science-fiction tale by Black-Sea Islander.

Black-Sea Islander had built up a reputation as a writer
who liked to hint at possessing quite intimate and somewhat
mysterious ties with the future. He often spoke in the future
tense, in a manner which intimated that he was merely a
guest in the present, a secret emissary from the future. He
behaved as though a spaceship from another world was waiting for him in some secluded spot at the edge of town. His
books sold well, but they always seemed a little long-winded
for me. More often than not, Black-Sea Islander depicted
the people of the future as being prone to obesity and complacency, concerned primarily with the satisfaction of their
excessive demands. As a person he seemed far more significant
than anything he had written. His virile and unusually reso-
lute face made a strong impression on me, as it had on everybody else.

I inquired among my friends about the dramatization
of his story. "A very original idea," they answered. "A person
meets himself in the future or the past. That Islander doesn't
mind playing cat-and-mouse with time."

Many of his readers liked his articles, which were written
in a bold style, as though he were attempting to open the
curtain which conceals the great riddle of the universe. Grey-
headed, but full of youthful romanticism and childlike

naiveté, he would walk into literary gatherings with a danc-ing gait, invariably bringing along all sorts of proof of his intimate ties with other worlds: fragments of meteorites, a glass tube containing dust particles from outer space, or a bone of a Mesozoic ant-eater, given to him by a paleontolo-gist friend. In his seventies, he dared to scale the icy heights of the highest mountains in search of the Abominable Snow-man. Even though he failed, he did enjoy renown and respect.

The greatest mystery was that television program. By what miracle was Black-Sea Islander able to peer into my childhood and dramatize my secret thoughts? And how could my past, the imagination of a science-fiction writer, and a mysterious book pedlar all cross paths?

The comments of my friends, who did not approve of the dramatization, left something unspoken and even ambiguous. Their guarded, furtive glances conveyed more than their words. My barber, though, was far more candid. "That was very clever acting," he said, "very clever. But there's one thing I can't understand. How in the world did you manage to get so small and play the part of that little boy, I mean yourself, but as a child?"

"Technique," I said, "a trick of the trade, a knack for transformation."

"The boy was a perfect double. At first I even thought he was your grandson. But it was something else, something even more strange."

"That's the way it was supposed to seem," I said. "It was a dramatization of a science-fiction story, a tale based on strictly scientific facts. Get it?"

"I'm trying to. What kind of tonic do you want, scented or unscented?"

3

Precisely at that time posters appeared all over the city announcing in huge letters a lecture by Black-Sea Islander, the famous writer of science fiction.

MEET THE STRANGER. FROM THE MARTIAN
SNOWS,
THE ABOMINABLE SNOWMAN.

The writer's face, deep in thought and perhaps slightly
melancholy, looked down from the posters at the passersby.
His expression promised even more than did the advertise-
ment.

I had difficulty in getting a ticket to "meet the stranger,"
even though a huge auditorium had been rented for the occasion. The spectators greeted the venerable writer with
applause, as he appeared on the stage carrying in his hand
a phial of effervescent liquid, the appearance of which suggested a strange, perhaps even other-worldly origin. He came
out, light on his feet for his age, almost dancing, looked
around and, suddenly standing on his tiptoes, uttered a word
which was most inappropriate for the occasion, considering
that he had just made his entrance and could not really be
thinking of disappearing into the wild blue yonder.

"Farewell," he said quietly and in a foreboding tone,
insinuating some special, hidden meaning in that word. Then
he paused and calmly, slowly, in a businesslike manner, began
to explain the unlikelihood of this wretched little word existing in any place but the sinful earth. He assumed, he said,
that the beings on other planets never said good-bye to
reality or to their friends and relatives, not wishing to betray
a spiritual weakness or to confess their frailty.

The audience listened to him as though everyone felt
that the bridge between the earth and outer space had
already been spanned. In Black-Sea Islander's voice were
heard hints of knowledge so intimate and thorough that he
had every right to share it with the audience.

"Our thought processes," he continued, "are witness
not only to the sagacity of the earthlings, but also to a
certain limitation of their imagination. In creating language
and designating by oral symbols everything located on this
side of the spiritual horizon, did humans have the right to

forget about possible encounters and contacts with representatives of another, extraterrestrial experience? Does this
not reveal a certain narrowness of view, the ethnocentric
nature of our language? Many years ago I set myself a task—
to create a language capable of linking mankind with another
spiritual milieu, with another mental environment. I compiled a stellar dictionary and reevaluated all of our earthly,
human conceptions. I observed myself, you and our entire
human world through the eyes of a stranger from out of
space. To achieve this I had to create new concepts, new
thought processes. With the aid of this new intellectual
equipment, with the help of this new, original language, I
transformed myself into an extraterrestrial being. Perceptive
readers have long been aware of this as they read my novels
and stories. In truth, my works are not merely information
about the unknown—they are a bridge which I have erected
between myself, the reader, and that what lurks beyond the
boundaries of the earthly biosphere, that which I have been
able to fathom, with the aid of the new logic which I created.
I would like to acquaint you with it after a brief recess. I
declare an intermission."

Making way through the thick crowd to the snack bar,
I spotted a table of books, numerous editions and reprints
of the novels and short stories by Black-Sea Islander. Selling
them was none other than my strange friend, the one who
looked like Dickens.

He offered me a book in a very colorful binding, the
title of which astonished me: *Stellar Dictionary: The Logic
of the Thought Processes of the Rational Beings on the
Planet N.*

"Is there such a planet?"

"Everything is possible in the boundless universe."

"Is it a novel or a philosophical treatise?"

"It's a combination of philosophy and flight of fancy."

"I'll take it."

"You'll find the book useful It's more than a book—it
contains a little something extra."

"You mean, life itself?" But the salesman was no longer paying any attention to me. He was busy with another customer.

4

The book was lying before me on the desk, and I was reading it. I was reading it? I had the feeling that the book was reading me, more than I was reading it. It was much too alive and active a book to calmly, gradually and thoroughly inform, edify and enlighten the reader. No, it was more like an extremely strange conversationalist—a telepathist, a hypnotist, a shrewd psychologist and analyst, imperceptibly and stealthily sizing up the reader. I had the feeling that there was someone in the room unseen, concealed between the pages of the book, blended in with the text.

The inquiring and inquisitive tone of Black-Sea Islander's narrative became more and more perceptible, more and more compelling as I read the book. It seemed that Black-Sea Islander himself was sitting beside me, holding the phial of effervescent liquid and examining me, sizing up my ability to relate to extraterrestrial reason. There was a chapter in the book which consisted of nothing but questions which a dweller in a distant civilization would be asking us earthlings. In a spare, graphic style the illustrator had depicted the sardonic examiner, giving him a most unearthly and forbidding appearance.

What did this emissary of unearthly reason ask me and the rest of mankind? At first glance the questions seemed strange, absurd, unexpected, accidental, not unlike a series of typographical errors. Why was I a biped? Why were not three ears and two noses specified in the genetic information which is coded in the chromosomes? Mentally I gave an evasive answer, alluding to the principles of expediency and comeliness.

Turning the page I found the answer, mockingly written by Black-Sea Islander as though he had foreseen my thoughts, evidence of stereotyped thinking. The unearthly examiner tried to confront me with the problems which scientists and philosophers had bypassed as a result of their earth-bound mentality and subjectivity.

Annoyed and uncomfortable, I closed the book and put it on the shelf. But I was irresistibly drawn to it, picked up the book again, and opened it. On the page to which it accidentally opened there was a drawing in which I was depicted, and alongside me stood a boy whom I recognized as myself.

What I read under the drawing did not deal with me, but the structure of time, the physical and psychic reality of which had been discovered by beings possessing otherworldly reason. It was amazing that a book which had nothing whatsoever to do with me used a drawing of me as an illustration. Having penetrated the secrets of the structure of time, an inhabitant of Planet N lived as though he were simultaneously projected into all stages of his existence. Childhood did not precede youth, youth—adulthood, adulthood—old age, but they all abided in a synchronic simultaneous existence.

The book was attempting to explain to me the essence of a phenomenon which does not yield to the logical processes at my disposal. It seemed the text was playing blindman's bluff with me. The drawing looked at me from the page, keeping me in a state of utter amazement, as though my life, too, were part of the text.

How did my picture get on that page, and especially in the form of an illustration for the conception of a synchronic, simultaneous existence? Could the book have been written solely for my benefit? But why? And, besides, as far as I can remember, there were several copies on the table. I glanced at the last page: "One hundred fifteen thousand copies in this printing."

It was uncanny. Putting on my coat and hat, I set out for a bookstore on Bolshoi Avenue where an acquaintance of mine, an elderly grey-haired saleswoman named Maria Stepanova, used to save certain limited editions for me. Behind the counter stood Dickens.

"What, you work here?" I asked.

"Yes. Maria Stepanova has retired and I have replaced her. He spoke calmly, in an ordinary, slow voice, and he wore an affectionate, slightly ambiguous smile, as though at once approving of me and censuring me. Of course, he already knew why I had come to the store.

An elderly woman walked up and Dickens, accomodating and efficient, showed her some new books. One of them caught her attention and she began to look through the illustrations. I felt the stare of the salesman on me. There was something guarded and yet playful about it. His stare drew my eyes to the page the old woman had opened. Glancing at it, I saw myself on the page. The old woman closed the book and said to the salesman, "Wrap it up. I'll take it."

A strange, wild sensation came over me when she handed the money to the salesman and took her purchase. It seemed to me that she was about to carry away a part of me. She left the store and went slowly on her way. Dickens leaned over and whispered: "There goes your past and future."

I rushed after the old woman, bumping into a little girl in the doorway, without even looking back. Everything flashed past, everything was hurrying, rushing like myself. A bus roared up. The old woman started to get on. I snatched the book from her arms. She screamed. I leaped aside. Several passersby rushed after me.

In the square I stopped to catch my breath. My professional appearance contradicted the obvious fact, but some civilian patrols came up and one of them asked to see my passport. I told him my academic rank. "I couldn't care less whether you're a professor. You snatched something from a senior citizen and tried to run away. Let me see your passport."

I handed it to him. Slowly and with great care he began to study my photo, which was attached to the document, then he transferred his guarded stare to me. In the photo I did not have a beard or a moustache, but the main difference was that I was fifteen years older.

Two fine lads, brimming with health and vitality, took me by the arms and led me to the police station. By their faces I could see that they were convinced they had captured a criminal of international renown who was impersonating a Ph.D. in history.

5

After looking over my documents and writing down the testimony of the civilian patrols, the man on duty, a blue-eyed lieutenant with a neat black moustache, ceremoniously opened the book, the material evidence of my criminal act. He looked at me, and then again at the illustration.

"How did you get in this book?"

"I don't know."

"Is this you or not?" I looked down and saw myself on the page, myself and the boy—also myself."

"Is it you, or not?"

"It is."

"Aha, and how did you get in a book about life in outer space? This seems to be a science-fiction novel."

"It is a novel."

"To tell the truth, the illustration is better proof of your identity than the passport. The passport photo doesn't really look like you."

"Maybe the novel is my real identification papers?"

"Save the jokes till later. Now we've got to establish your identity and find out how this book wound up in your possession."

I kept silent.

"I am prepared to accept that the book accidentally wound up in your possession. But why did you start running?"

"I stopped as soon as the patrolmen called out to me."

"Granted. But this book—does it belong to you or to that senior citizen?"

"Aren't you forgetting something much more important?" I asked.

"Namely?"

"How did my picture get in the book?"

The lieutenant frowned. "But it might not be a picture of you."

"Then whose is it?"

"Probably of the fellow described in the novel."

"Well, take another look."

The lieutenant began to thumb through the pages, but he could not find the illustration. It was not there, and I somehow knew he would not find it. I felt it in my bones. I had the feeling that it wasn't the picture that was being hunted, but I, myself.

"What the devil . . ." said the lieutenant as though to himself. "That picture—was it here, or not?" His face suddenly looked tired, like after a sleepless night. "You still have to prove your identity," he said, suddenly angry.

"Call the institute where I work."

"I'll have time for that later. But you explain to me why you took somebody else's book, and why you're trying to assume somebody else's identity. Do you mean to pass yourself off as the hero of the novel?"

"You must explain the presence and then the subsequent disappearance of the illustration. Besides, why were you, a prosperous man, tempted by this book? Why do you refuse to give straightforward answers and try to hide behind this novel?"

"I'm not trying to hide behind this book. Someone else is . . . ."

"Exactly who? Be specific."

"Dickens."

"Dickens? Assuming that's true, let's have the whole story from the beginning."

Patiently and avoiding superfluous details, I told him all that had happened to me, beginning with my acquaintance with the strange salesman and ending with the encounter with the old lady.

Again he started thumbing through the book, slowly, carefully, scrutinizing each page. I watched his fingers, hoping that the illustration would reappear in its place. He turned the last page and sighed audibly, "What a mess! This is a fine kettle of fish. I can't explain anything to my superior, or even to myself."

I recalled the contents of the book and thought: "A police lieutenant, a captive representative of earthly logic, naturally is stumped by this puzzling phenomenon."

As though guessing my thoughts, the lieutenant asked, "Do you know the contents of the book?"

"I'm familiar with it," I answered. "It's a sort of test."

"Every book is a test. That is, of course if it is ideologically consistent and its function is to educate."

"This book has a special function."

"What's that?"

"To have everyone flunk the test—you, me, and all the rest of mankind."

The lieutenant laughed "More likely you're the one who'd give everybody an 'F'. A book is kind. No editor would publish an ill-tempered book."

"Ill-tempered books are also necessary."

"Depends on who needs them. Disturbers of the peace, maybe. Let's get back to business. You still haven't convinced me."

"Look through it again and see."

His face looked tired and suspicious. "Frankly, I'm beginning to doubt that it ever was there."

Once again he started thumbing through the book. Suddenly an expression of joyful surprise lighted up his face. "Look! It turned up again. Here it is in its place." He showed me the illustration. "The pages were stuck together. That's what was the matter."

The lieutenant was happy, as though he had straightened things out. I, too, was happy that the picture had turned up.

To tell the truth, I wasn't at all sure that it wouldn't disappear again. The lieutenant also seemed to fear this, and didn't close the book, but kept his palm firmly on the open page. He was carefully inspecting the drawing, comparing it with me.

"Of course, there's a resemblance," he said, "but that's immaterial. The artist liked your looks, so he drew you without your knowledge and then used that sketch as an illustration in this novel. Right?" The logic and consistency of this theory obviously pleased him and, even though it didn't convince me, I did not protest.

"Well," said the lieutenant, "that about wraps it up. I could hardly suspect a distinguished scholar of malicious intent. You can go now. I'll keep the book in case the woman who lost it comes back for it."

He smiled, still not taking his hand off the open page, as though afraid the drawing would disappear again. "Go on home. And try not to get involved in situations that are difficult to explain. Try to see it from our point of view."

6

Upon returning home, I retired to my study and began reading Black-Sea Islander's book of science fiction. From the very first page I found the novel strange and ambiguous and throbbing as an organism from the depths of a sea on a distant planet. I felt I was face-to-face with a visitor from Planet N, who somehow established an intimate and mysterious contact with me. I soon regretted that I was not a philosopher, so that I could carry on an intellectual discussion without putting my foot into my mouth. From the vantage point of his lofty spiritual and social experience, this otherworldly philosopher was now interrogating me as though he were questioning not me alone, but the basic principles of human logic.

"Time, you say?" he almost shouted at me. "Be so kind as to explain what that is."

I muttered something about the irrevocability of time and about the fact that, in relation to the future, the present is always the past. But since he was thoroughly conversant with the laws of time, everything I said seemed as naive and amusing as Neanderthal man's observations on the essence of quantum mechanics.

Life creates order out of chaos. No doubt? But each man's life has always depended on time and its inflexible boundaries between the beginning and the end. Because the inhabitants of Planet N have mastered the laws of nature, they learned how to circumvent the straightforward movement of time. Thus, if he wishes, an adult can carry on a conversation with a young person or a child by perceiving himself in the child and adjusting himself in time as in space. My knowledge of mathematics was not broad enough to understand the principle of conversion of time into space, a unique type of space—fluctuating and dynamic, but nevertheless not unidirectional—which aligned all the correlatives of multisynchronism in a single focal point.

My head had already begun to spin a little from the mental effort I was expending on trying to comprehend something which contradicted all laws of earthly, human logic, when I came across an episode from my own childhood. My schoolteacher, Nikolai Alexandrovich, called to me from the pages of that amazing book, sending me to the geography map, the same one we had in 1919. Outside was the spring and the trees and the sky of my childhood, and the sun, big and bright, not at all like the sun nowadays. With incomprehensible mastery a link was now made between me and what had disappeared without a trace. I stood in the classroom beside the geography map, and my heart was pounding and my ears were ringing with thousands of thoughts and desires which came back to me along with my childhood and my teacher who was looking at me with the boundless curiosity of a man who is looking into a child's future. I was silent but Nikolai Alexandrovich talked and talked, addressing himself not to me, but to my future.

The page ended and the vision vanished. And I sat there amazed that Black-Sea Islander could link my past, my distant childhood, to his plot. How could he know what I alone knew? I closed the book, feeling that I was closing the door to my childhood. Inexplicably, I felt a strong urge to see Dickens. I found him in the book shop.

"How's business? I asked.

"Could be better. Everybody's asking for Black-Sea Islander, but his books are all sold out."

"Nothing left? Not even for me?"

Lowering his voice to a whisper, he answered, "I saved one copy, I knew you would want the book."

"Does it have the illustration?"

"What illustration?"

"The same one that. . . ."

"Let's see." He reached for the book, and started looking for the drawing, but it was not there, He looked up at me and curiosity shone on his lean, intelligent face, as though he really expected me to explain the extraordinary phenomenon to him.

"Somebody is making me see things in this book that aren't there."

"Somebody? He laughed. "I can guess who."

"Who?"

"I."

"But Planet N is Black-Sea Islander's brain-child."

"You are mistaken. Not even Black-Sea Islander himself suspects that his gifted pen is a bridge between two civilizations, that his novels are in many ways documentaries."

"How do you know that?"

"I'm his coauthor. We use his style and my facts."

7

When I got home I found a man waiting for me. It was the same police lieutenant who had interrogated me. His face was taut, severe, and distrustful. He was standing by the wall, fixedly gazing at a print of Van Gogh's famous painting "Night Café." He did not take his intensely curious eyes off the painting, as though his presence had some connection with the unusual, alarming and tragic theme of the work.

He greeted me by nodding his head and said, "I came about that book. I have it with me." He pulled out of his bag a book that was carefully wrapped in a white sheet of drafting paper.

"It's an evil book, strange and evil."

"What makes you say this?"

"Your picture is gone, and my image has appeared in its place."

"What do I have to do with it?"

"I want to straighten this thing out before I report to my superiors."

"Why report it altogether? Maybe you merely thought you saw a picture of yourself."

He opened the book and showed me the illustration. I saw an image of a boy with an animated, laughing face.

"But that's some young boy," I said.

"No, that's me as a child. Exactly the same picture is hanging on a wall at home. But it wasn't there before. It appeared after you left."

"Perhaps it was there, though," I said "Maybe the pages were stuck together, and we didn't notice it."

"Granted, but how did I get there, and as a child? Explain that."

"Some phenomena are simply inexplicable. We have to wait until science explains them."

"I can't wait. My job is the kind that doesn't allow for confusion. It won't stand for disorder."

"For goodness sake, what do you mean, 'disorder?' This is a book—an intellectual novel. So, a misprint slipped in. Your picture accidentally got into the text."

"That's hard to believe," the lieutenant objected. "First your picture, then mine. I've got to figure this thing out. I didn't sleep a wink last night. I was counting on you, and you're letting me down."

"I'm not letting you down. Believe me, I know little more than you. I think we have to look for the solution in the contents of the book itself. Have you read it?"

"Twice in a row."

"Didn't the contents seem strange to you?"

"I didn't find anything strange. It's fantasy. Except there's too much science in it."

"But this science is not ours, not the earthly kind. . . ."

"I didn't come here to discuss a novel with you. It's these pictures. . . ." He waved his hand in despair.

"You know, I think someone is playing games with both of us."

"Yes, someone. But I've got to find out who that someone is. Have you spoken to the author."

"Not yet. But I shall. I'll let you know if I find out anything."

8

When I called on an old friend from my college days, I hardly suspected that I would again be confronted with this riddle which had already tortured me for several days.

"What do you think of Black-Sea Islander's works?" asked my friend's daughter, a college student.

I answered quietly so as not to attract the attention of the other guests seated around the table. "In science fiction I prefer something simple, something easily understood by a person who dreams of a tranquil existence. Besides, Black-Sea Islander. . . . What gives him the right to act as the intermediary between us and the future?"

"Talent."

"And exactly what is talent?" I asked the student. On her face I noticed a shade of confusion and bewilderment, as though she were stumped on an examination. "Talent," I continued, "is a brilliant gift, brimming with joy as it manifests itself. But in the works of your Islander I see nothing joyful. What does he seek to impart us? Knowledge of the highly enlightened beings on other planets? He depicts them in such a way that they frighten me."

Black-Sea Islander will be interested to hear this. As a matter of fact, we expect him here any minute now. I'm going to write my senior thesis about him."

"So, you must be an authority on his works, and, no doubt, his biography, too. Where was he born?" At this point the bell rang. It was he—Black-Sea Islander himself.

"Greetings," he said, and theatrically raised his hand. Then he pressed it to his heart. The college girl introduced me to him and I said: "Your reader, and . . . admirer." I blushed like a boy. I was not at all his admirer. On the contrary, everything he wrote seemed vulgar to me. But he was already looking down at me with the condescending stare reserved for admirers. I could not resist an attempt to take him down a peg or two, and asked quietly and pointedly, "How's Dickens getting along?"

"For a split second he looked dumbfounded, but quickly regained his composure. "Dickens? Well, for that matter I prefer Poe or Jules Verne, but the objective laws of truth prevent me from conveying their greetings to you. They are back there in the past, and we are here at this lovely table."

"I'm not talking about the Dickens who wrote *Dombey and Son*. . . . Who is that other Dickens?"

"Who is he? Who am I? Who are you?" The writer moved over to the college girl. "You, Gertie, I would never ask, 'Who are you?' You are a sweet, kind creature. In your presence everything takes its proper place, everything becomes kind and clear and understandable, even the incomprehensive and the enigmatic."

9

Sociologists predict that in a thousand years the entire population of our planet will consist exclusively of scholars.

Is that good or bad? I don't know and keep wondering about what those people will be like. If the relationships between them will be like those between myself and two of my graduate students, named Belousov and Mokrosheiko, that would be almost catastrophic. To them I am something like a walking reference book, a man crammed full of information and facts. Rather than consult a book they consult my memory. An examination is a different matter. There, I ask the questions, and they give the answers. I judge them by their answers, but then they also judge me by my questions.

During my many years of work I have grown accustomed to evaluating people by what they know and how well they know it. I have taught myself to look upon life as though it were standing at the door, waiting for its turn to take my examination. The thought that the entire population of the planet might consist of no one but scholars upsets me. A million Mokrosheikos and Belousovs, but how many like Seregin? Hundreds, or only a few? Once I asked Seregin if he indulges in introspection. "Introspection?" he laughed. Auguste Comte ridiculed introspection as a foolish attempt of man to look out the window and see himself walking along the street. Yet, how I would love to look out the window and see myself."

"But that's not possible."

"I always seem to want the impossible. I suffer because man cannot transcend the limits of the possible. For example, I know that even if I live to be ninety, I will never exchange words with a representative of another system of logic, another extraterrestrial experience. The distance is too vast."

"I don't understand your longing," I said. "Earthly, ordinary companions are quite satisfactory for me. When I have the desire to communicate with some higher intellect, I open a volume of Pushkin, Hegel, or Goethe."

"That's not enough for me," said Seregin. "They are great, of course, but their thinking processes are the same as our own, earthbound. And I would like to become acquainted with another system borne of another milieu.

The realization that this is impossible drives me alternately to despair and rage."

"But why?"

"Our entire civilization is directed toward a dialogue between ourselves and those to whom we refer as 'you'. 'I', 'we,' cannot exist without 'you.' The earthlings humanity cannot always remain a Robinson Crusoe on its tiny planet-island. Just so that he could say 'you,' and hear 'you' in return, Crusoe trained a parrot. Without a dialogue with another system of logic our whole human culture is merely a parrot, an illusion, self-deception."

"I don't quite understand your point, Seregin. Mankind is billions of individuals in continuous association with each other. How can you compare mankind with Robinson Crusoe?"

"We're talking about two different things. The laws of logic, the laws of the thought process, unite one and all, form a single whole. Logic cannot be individual. Only logic relates people to each other."

"So you admit the possibility of another logic which has nothing in common with ours?"

"Why not?"

"Is this then," I asked Seregin, "why you are so interested in the problems of communication, in semantics, and in the languages and thought processes of ancient and primitive peoples?"

"Yes." I had always been aware of Seregin's strangeness. Dreaming of the impossible, he had always seemed like a modern Faust to me. And I always sensed in him the potential for contact with another world, another milieu, another dimension.

10

One day Seregin called on me. He had a book in his hand. His face wore an expression of mock amazement, as though he had just witnessed something extraordinary.

"What is it?" I asked. "Did you just see yourself by looking out the window?"

"Not myself—you."

"Where?"

"In a book that has nothing to do with you. In a science-fiction novel by Black-Sea Islander."

"Where did you buy the book?"

"In a bookstore on Bolshoi Avenue, from a handsome, elegantly old-fashioned salesman who looks sort of like Dickens."

"That explains everything," I muttered.

"And I am completely dumbfounded. What is your picture doing in a science-fiction novel?" He opened the book to show me the sketch of myself. As I expected, it had disappeared. Seregin pleaded for some explanation.

"I am no more than a sign, a letter, a hieroglyph," I told him. "My image is a symbol by means of which a representative from an extraterrestrial system of thought seeks to establish logical contact with you."

"It's a joke!"

"I'm dead serious."

"Then where is he?"

"A short walk from here."

"Dozens of light years away?"

"Oh, no! He's right here, on Bolshoi Avenue, in the same store where you bought the book."

"You don't mean that salesman, the one who was flaunting his preposterous chance resemblance to Dickens?"

"I don't think the resemblance is accidental."

"You mean he's an actor made up like Dickens?"

"No, more likely a director of genius, or a god who created himself and his partner, Black-Sea Islander, as well. But, it's better for you to learn all this first hand. Extraterrestrial reason has made contact with you through the illustration."

Seregin once again opened the book and his face turned pale. "Look, it seems to be me."

Yes, it was he, as though he had been suddenly repro-
duced. He was standing beside me and also on the page of
the book—not as an illustration, but alive, though immensely
reduced in size. We both looked in horror at that strange
phenomenon. A minute dragged by as though it were an
eternity. Then, gradually, Seregin's diminutive duplicate
turned back into an illustration and merged with the page.

"It's a mirage! An hallucination! An optical illusion!"
said Seregin, addressing me not so much as himself.

"But, that's not all," I objected. It's something else,
something more than that."

"Exactly what?"

"Ask the fellow you bought the book from."

Seregin seized the book and dashed off at a run.

I did not see him until three days later. He had lost
weight, obviously from lack of sleep.

"How did it go?" I asked. "Did you talk to him? Did
he give you an explanation?"

Seregin laughed. "It's all nonsense, confusing, illogical.
It's one thing to have a conversation, but who was I conversing with?"

"It isn't that hard to recognize him."

"Very hard."

"But he looks like Dickens."

"Dickens? Right now he's a dead ringer for Chekhov—
Van Dyke beard, pince-nez on a ribbon. Even his height has
changed."

"Whatever for?"

"How should I know? He was polite and cordial, but
the whole time I felt that the counter was between us, and
that something else, invisible, yet impenetrable, was separat-
ting us."

"What did he say?"

"He said that he doesn't write books, but merely sells
them. He advised me to inquire of Black-Sea Islander about
his novel and he asked me to excuse him. He said he was at
work, and had neither the time nor the right to carry on

private conversations. I approached him several more times, pretending to be interested in some new books, but be gave me such a look that I was embarrassed. Maybe he does not actually have anything to do with this phenomenon. Maybe it's some peculiar feature of Black-Sea Islander's talent."

"What do you mean?"

"Of course, I don't believe in magic or sorcery. But, suppose he's a telepathist or a hypnotist."

"But we weren't reading—we were simply watching the strange phenomenon as it occurred."

"True."

"You say he resembles Chekhov now?"

"An exact copy, a double."

"I'll go down there after dinner and look at him myself."

I dropped by the bookstore not long before closing time. The salesman's appearance really had changed.

"Hello, Dickens," I said quietly and slowly.

"You mean I still look like Dickens?" he asked.

"Well, no. Now, perhaps you look more like Chekhov."

"Does it strike one immediately?"

"Not right away, but it does. . . . Your facial expression has changed. It's pensively intelligent—in the style of the 1890s."

"Lately I've been engrossed in Chekhov. I tried to understand the essence of his artistic philosophy, of his ordinary heroes. And, you see, under the influence. . . . Unlike you earthlings, we are too impressionable, like children."

11

Some contemporary historian said of written lai uage that it is a special art which has enriched man's conscio ness of the philosophical simultaneity of all the generations. nd, in truth, the written language is my area of specializa n. Nevertheless, I have never experienced such anxiety, suc. a fear of contact with another way of life through signs and characters, as Seregin was experiencing. It was as though he were born to exist in the present and in the past simultaneously, to hear the voices of centuries and of generations, with the aid of hieroglyphs and of even more ancient signs, to become a part of that which unites people in a harmonious, eternal union of history and life. The philosophical unity of generations might seem to be a complete victory over time, yet it is not. Signs and characters open the door to the past, but the door to the future nevertheless remains closed. It will be opened only when mankind makes contact with extraterrestrial rationality, and not before.

This thought gave Seregin no peace, especially now that extraterrestrial rationality had manifested itself, choosing as its intermediary the book salesman in the shop on Bolshoi Avenue. A miracle was taking place before our very eyes, but Seregin didn't believe it, and in fact I, too, believed it only at times, when the image appeared and disappeared on the pages of Black-Sea Islander's novel.

A month passed, then two more. Everything seemed to be going well. Whenever I looked into a book, I saw in it only what was printed—nothing else. Seregin also opened new books without fear and without the expectation of learning something contradictory to common sense. From time to time we would drop into the store on Bolshoi Avenue to look at the salesman who continued to resemble Chekhov, and also Dickens. Each time we pretended to have come to the store simply to make sure we did not miss some interesting new publication. And, indeed, we displayed an excessive interest in everything that lay on the counter.

On hot, humid days the salesman piled books on a folding table out on the street, never failing to draw an excited crowd. "Doesn't it seem to you," Seregin asked me in a low voice, glancing at the salesman, "that he is the very spirit of knowledge, the spirit of writing and printing, that he is a living personification of the link between generations?"

"No, it doesn't," I answered. Seregin looked at me inquisitively. "No, he has been summoned," I continued, "to bring together not generations, but two systems of thought, two systems of logic—ours and the one that empowered him."

"Nonsense," Seregin interrupted me, "I don't believe it. Even you don't believe what you're saying. He's a hypnotist, a telepathist, a talented magician who is adept at playing with other people's perception."

"Then why does he sell books?"

"He is a book lover!" insisted Seregin. "Such people used to go off to a monastery and shut themselves up in a cell so they would communicate with God in private. Now the book itself has become god. It has replaced faith. It's a refuge for austere, ascetic souls."

The salesman caught sight of us and beckoned us with a look. "I think I have something for you," he said softly, "a translation from the English. I believe both of you are interested in semantics and symbols? This is just the thing for you." And he handed us *A History of Signs and Symbols.* "Unfortunately, there's only one copy." I let Seregin have it, pretending that I was already familiar with the book.

12

Several days passed before I saw Seregin again. He came in the evening, wearing an absent-minded, almost vacant expression on his face.

"Where have you been?" I asked.

"You wouldn't believe it if I told you."

"Where?"

"In the past. Not in my past, but in that book seller's past. He keyed me into his memory and made it possible for me to see the world through his eyes. Even now it seems to me that he and I are the same person. But there is one thing about it that keeps disturbing me."

"What's that?"

"The impossibility of merging these two worlds that are now coexisting in my consciousness."

"Calm down. Tell me the whole story from the beginning."

"All right," he said. Where should I begin? In my consciousness all the beginnings and the ends have gotten entangled. . . . Don't interrupt me. I had overcome the barrier, that invisible something which stood between him and me. He invited me over to his place. Nothing extraordinary—a staircase, a door, a mailbox. He turned the key and we found ourselves in a room that looks like thousands of others."

'Who are you?' I asked.

'Sergei Tikhonovich Spiridonov,' he answered. 'Yes, I have a first name, a patronymic, and surname, like everybody else who lives in this town. But, besides that, I have something that no one else has—the knowledge of life here, multiplied by the experience of my own civilization. . . .'

'Cut it out,' I interrupted him 'You'd better tell me what makes you assume this absurd role of "stranger"? It's dull and vulgar, calculated to appeal to immature adolescents who've read too much of the Black-Sea Islander and his likes.'

'All right, then,' he said, 'call me Seryozha. And if you'll allow me, I'll call you Valya. A Seryozha couldn't have come from another world. Let's have a drink and a bite to eat, and a heart to heart talk.'

From a walnut case he took a bottle of cognac and some candy and we drank. 'I love the ordinary, the commonplace. Mind you, your great writers valued it highly, too, especially Chekhov. Sometimes I hate myself for having chosen to sell books, when it would have been so much more ordinary to sell soap, toothbrushes or buttons. Let's drink to the commonplace, Valya! I know that the esoteric appeals to you— Egyptian hieroglyphics, Japanese characters, the inscriptions found on Easter Island. To hell with that. People need the ordinary, the boredom of a train station in the heat of summer, and small talk over tea. Or cognac.' We clicked glasses. The drink went to my head.

'Forget your hieroglyphics and the history of writing,' he went on. 'That's all nonsense. Mankind was happier before it learned to read and write. The Old Testament legend about the Tree of Knowledge of good and evil has great beauty. You don't believe me? You shouldn't. I don't even believe myself. I want to become a man, don't you see? But what makes man is not quantum mechanics, not biophysics, but the ordinary things in life, one's habits. Take habits away from man, and he becomes an abstraction, an x or a y. Can you guess why I feel such longing for the ordinary?'

'I wish I could.'

'Because I'm from another world. This sounds absurd, ridiculous, doesn't it? But it's the truth. I am actually a symbol, an hieroglyph. I was created for communication. You don't believe it, I see, but in half an hour you will, after I acquaint you with nature. First you own, earthly nature which you and everyone else, even your poets and artists, do not really see, and then I'll acquaint you with my distant world. I'll key you into my consciousness.'

Out of a desk drawer he took a small gadget that looked like an electric razor and switched it on. At the same moment I became aware of a feeling I used to have in childhood when I jumped naked into a freezing river and gasped for breath. I seemed to be enveloped by space. Everything in me expanded, broadened, and was blissfully released.

'You are a river,' I heard a voice say. 'Flow, rush along, surge forth.' And I did feel like a river, and the shore was far, far away. Carried along, I saw my free transparent body. I grew broader and larger, released from everything that I had been. My eyes and ears confirmed what my body felt, stretched out for hundreds of kilometers, existing here and far away at the same time.

In the blue of the cold currents, in the ripples of the waves, in the flowing, rushing element which was enveloping the free expance of the river bed, I experienced the strange unity of eternity and an instant. I saw hilly shores, forests, and roads, and clouds, reflected in my transparent blue, lazily floated by. In the glow of the summer sky above me I saw a swallow, giddy from the free expanses, darting to and fro on its small, strong wings, playing with the air, plunging downward, yet not really falling supported by the bouyant, transparent blue.

I was free, and there was neither an end nor a beginning to my freedom. Everything in me expanded like after waking up early in the morning in childhood. The world was breathlessly new. It was fresh and primordial, like that larch on the shore, reflected in the water preening itself, watching in amazement its dark, almost black branches which smelled of resin and the combined odor of summer heat and the almost icy cold of the flowing river that was I. I was like a mirrow, as I was for the forests, which slowly stretched along the shores and formed a cool canopy over me. Over me. On one side there were birches, and on the other side there were firs and pines, and my swift body, bearing itself along, carrying its watery might, joined and separated the forests and groves like a never-ending song.

My childhood was with me: the murmur of the stream that was the beginning of a river and ended in the sea. But it was no ordinary beginning—it never ended. And it was no ordinary end, for it began over and over again. I carried fishing boats and steamers full of passengers, rocking them like a cradle, rocking and pitching. And the shores grew further and further apart, playing some enchanting game with space.

'What a river! oh, what a river!' exclaimed a youth to the girl standing beside him on the deck of a passenger ship.

'Speak softly,' said the girl, 'the river can hear us.'

The voices vanished in the distance with my movements. Then the windows of the homes on shore lighted up. Quiet set in.

'You weren't having a dream, Valya' said the one who called himself Sergei Spiridonov, 'you were seeing the world the way *we* see it. Once upon a time, in the remote era of myths and fairy tales, man was one with nature, in close unity with the forests and lakes. But then, civilization severed the umbilical cord. Our civilization, in contrast to yours, has maintained it, losing nothing. Our senses kept pace with the expanding reason, instead of being left, like some game, in the hands of children, savages and poets. You were not a river. The river was you. It poured into your feelings and carried you along. Do you regret it?'

'I regret that I woke up too soon.'

'You wanted to remain a river forever? But rivers are mortal, too. People poison them with chemical refuse. Besides, you were not a river—you had merged with the river at the moment of recognition. I brought you into contact with our vision, our logic, you dreamed of becoming acquainted with another type of thought. But you turned out to be too naive. You identified yourself with the object you were thinking about.'

'Who are you?'

'An emissary, an intermediary who picked you out of several billions of earthlings to enter into a dialogue. For hundreds of thousands of years your earthly reason has, in fact, been conversing with itself, without being aware of any other logic besides that which merged millions into what is called humanity. But now you, a human, are talking with me. The two systems of logic, earthly and extraterrestrial, have made contact.'

'But this isn't your first day on earth! You even have an earthly profession. When you are selling books, you talk with the customers.'

'That's an entirely different mater, Valya. I talk with them in their language. I answer the most elementary questions. But our dialogue, mine and yours, began the moment you felt the expanse of the river's current. . . .'

'Dialogue? Is that what you call it? But you were silent. And I was silent, too. Only nature was speaking.'

'You are mistaken. That was my conversation with you about your surroundings. Thought linked us with motion, with the course of nature herself.'

'But the sketch in the book, my picture that kept appearing and disappearing?'

'That was a practical joke, Valya. Don't be angry. It was merely a way of reminding you that there are other methods of information and communication besides those known on earth. But don't think I didn't profit by that game, selling books. I was searching for a person suitable for the dialogue.'

'But why did you select a humble graduate student rather than a renowned scholar?'

'I observed you and your attitudes. I watched you as you opened a book and became intoxicated with the revelations of its secret. One of your earthling scientists has said that philosophy is the unravelling of the world's mysteries. I will help you to decipher what your conquerors of earthly secrets never even dreamed of. No one knows who I am, except for you, your adviser and hapless writer of science fiction to whom I occasionally throw a bone out of the warehouse of the future.'

'Why are you collaborating with Black-Sea Islander?'

'What do you mean, why? I wish to help him. I can depend on his discretion. It's not in his interest to reveal the secret of his anonymous coauthor. That would be like cutting off your nose to spite your face. I've been his nose for many years, ever since I landed here on earth. Sometimes he simply types what I dictate. And then he reads the text aloud, as though he had written it all himself.'

'I don't understand you, Seryozha. You are almost god-like. You were able to turn me into a river and then convince me that it didn't really happen. But when you dictate to that seventy-year-old simpleton, can't you pass on some original idea to him?'

'I try not to stand out from the crowd. Earthlings call it modesty.'

'Don't you mistake banality for modesty.'

He laughed. 'You better go home. I'm sleepy.'

'See you tomorrow,' I said, as I got up to leave.

'No, we have to bide our time for a few days, so you can prepare yourself, Valya.'

'For what?'

'For an encounter with what you earthlings, steeped in the commonplace, would consider impossible.'

Seregin continued his story:

And that encounter took place. Once more he opened the desk drawer and took out the gadget that resembled an electric razor and looked at me with the searching stare of a doctor. At that moment, everything that I ever knew and loved was suddenly severed from me by a thousand light years, opening an abyss between me and my native land. Similar sensations happen only in a dream, when something alien merges with your existence. I reminisced nostalgically: there, infinitely far away, were my wife and two children. And I would never see them again. The distance was too great and fathomless.

A new present enters my life. I hear music. An invisible orchestra is performing a symphony. A young woman walks up to me. 'You've grown thin, my dear,' she says. 'Look in the mirror.' She gives me a tiny hand mirror. It is alive and transparent. It is a miniature forest lake, framed by a metal rim. I look in it and my pale face ripples, reflected in the dark blue water of that strange, real-life lake.

'Who are you?' I ask.

'Your wife, Nedrigana, my darling. How did you manage to forget me in these few short days?'

'But I'm not married. I never was.'

'And what about the two children you left behind in the farthest reaches of space when you set off on this expedition. Have you forgotten about them so soon? Are you trying to get used to the idea that you don't have a family? The vast distances will inevitably make you forget it.'

'I've never been married.'

'You mean, you're getting used to the idea that you won't return?'

'No,' I answered, 'I will go back.'

'You will return, my dear. We will wait years. Year after year we shall wait for you. You must return.'

I rise and follow her to a picture hanging on the wall. It is a living fragment of nature, a small part of nature placed in a frame. An orchard stirs inside it, green branches rustling with the wind. At first I seem to be looking through a window. But a window would have given more of a feeling of distance, since it would have been cut out of the wall toward the living expanse of nature. But this is different. The grove is inside me, and also beside me, in the frame, like that forest lake into which I had been staring a few minutes ago.

'You are saying farewell to things, my dear. I understand. But why don't you find a few words to say to me, words I could remember when you are far away? Do say something.'

I am silent. I am overwhelmed by the realization of some incalculable loss, as if, for the opportunity of participating in this expedition, I am paying with everything that is dear to me—my family, friends, history, and, finally, the whole biosphere of the planet.

'My darling,' I heard, 'all this time you've been preparing for your disappearance. Forgive me for referring in this manner to an expedition to a distant planet which does have something in common with us and where, according to our scientists, reality is reasonable and reason is realistic. But somehow, I'm fearful of that reason, although, of course, the infinite spaces that will engulf you are even more frightening. My darling, oh, my dear, we had years at our disposal, but they are gone, and now only numbered minutes are left. Let us stop time, if you wish, let us retard its flow, to deceive our tense feelings. But, no, you are silent.'

I am silent, not because of the dramatic tension of those minutes before the parting, but because of something else— the awkward realization that I am an outsider, that I am being taken for someone else.

Then, abruptly, everything ended. It all came to a sudden

stop. Once again I was beside Seryozha near the table where a bottle of cognac was standing.

'Did all this really happen?' I asked

'It did, but it happened to me, not you. You saw a fragment of my life.'

I believed him, and yet I didn't believe him. And when Seregin left me, I felt something akin to envy. It was stupid envy, illogical and absurd. Or was it? I envied this graduate student who writing a thesis for me, had been chosen for contact with another reality. As for myself, that reality was merely teasing me by playing games with my picture, making it disappear and then appear again. It was teasing me and along with me the ever-logical police lieutenant.

13

No sooner had I remembered the lieutenant than he dropped by my apartment.

"Excuse me for bothering you," said the lieutenant. "I've come about that, uh . . . about that disturbance of the peace."

"As far as I can see, I'm the one who disturbed the peace."

"You? No, I don't think so. I came about that incident with the drawing. Did it really take place?"

"Which would you rather—yes or no?"

"Life doesn't always take our wishes into consideration. I reported the incident to my superiors, but they didn't believe me. They're sending me to a neuropathologist for examination. 'You're overtired,' that's what they said. It might help matters if you would confirm the fact."

"What makes you think they'd believe me?"

"You're a distinguished scholar."

"What do you want me to do?"

"Call on my section chief and confirm my story about the drawing."

"That's possible. But, then, I'll have to go to the neuro-pathologist. What would I say to him?"

"Tell him everything, exactly the way it was."

"What if he doesn't believe me?"

"Give him my telephone number."

"How would that help? He'd either suspect that we're both crazy, or that it's a trick. Either one is bad for me. I was on duty, in the first place. I was making an investigation, in the second place."

I was amazed at Police Lieutenant Avdeichev's flawless logic. It was logic based on the whole of man's experience on earth. But there also existed another logic, about which the lieutenant and, for that matter, his stern superior, knew nothing.

"They won't fire you, I'm sure," I said.

"They could easily fire me. The doctor could say that I'm either sick or tried to pull a fast one."

"We need a couple of days. I'll inquire of some national-ly known specialists."

"We can bide our time for a couple of days, but no more," said the lieutenant, getting up from his chair. "A couple of days," he repeated. "So, I'll drop in on you next week."

He paused in the hall, mulling something over in his mind, and said, "A couple of days—a lot of water can go over the dam in that time. Including a nervous breakdown. Oh well, see you later."

A couple of days—one hardly has time to turn around before they're gone. We needed more than a couple of days—we needed a couple of years, or maybe decades. After all, the incident concerned the most significant, the most para-doxical event in the whole history of human knowledge. I thought of this as soon as the door shut behind the police lieutenant. And then another thought occurred to me. Does he have a wife and children? And how terrible it would be if they fired him. I felt responsible for the lieutenant's fate. He released me after I had been detained by the civilian patrols, released me, trusting in his flawless logic, in his common sense and the dictates of his kind heart.

I telephoned Seregin. Half an hour later he was sitting in my study, wrapped in cigarette smoke and listening to me. By the expression on his face, which had suddenly become cautiously mocking, I saw that the lieutenant's fate did not interest him in the least.

"They'll put him on part-time," Seregin said. He won't be ruined. He'll find another job, and that's that."

"With a certificate stating that he's psychologically unbalanced?"

"We must not get the police involved in this. We might jeopardize mankind's chance for contact with an emissary from another biosphere, another system of logic."

"Would it really hinder contact if the police learn that a salesman in a bookstore on Bolshoi Avenue, is combining his real profession with another one? After all, the business of selling books is honest work, devoted to reason and progress."

At that point the telephone rang and I picked up the receiver. A man was saying in an exceptionally polite, even somewhat ingratiating voice:

"I beg your indulgence. Circumstances of truly global proportions have made it imperative for me to interrupt your profound meditations, even, perhaps, your research in the field of semantics and the history of known systems. Yes, circumstances of truly global. . . ."

"Who is speaking?" I interrupted the mighty flow of words.

"Black-Sea Islander speaking. I absolutely must see you."

"Why not? Drop over this evening. I'll be at home."

I didn't tell Seregin who called me, but he had obviously guessed.

"Our bookseller Seryozha hasn't been in a very good mood lately," he said.

"How come?"

"A quarrel with Black-Sea Islander. It was he who just called you, wasn't it?"

"How did you guess?"

"Intuition. I'm slightly afraid of him. No, not for myself —for Seryozha. The man's been intimating to him that he can no longer hide from society and science such a 'global' fact. Global is his favorite word."

"What advantage can there be in that for him? Hasn't Seryozha been helping him?"

"Not any more. He categorically refused. And Black-Sea Islander hasn't been able to. . . ."

"Why did he refuse?"

"I talked him into it."

"You shouldn't have done that, butting into other people's affairs. Now you'll have to get yourself out of it. This is a more serious matter than the Lieutenant."

"It's too late to talk about that now. It's already done."

"But you must convince him that he can't leave Black-Sea Islander in the lurch. Islander serves a useful purpose, instills in young people a thirst for knowledge, inspires them to flights of fantasy and dreams."

"Phooey! Your Black-Sea Islander is interested in nothing but royalties!"

And with that Seregin disappeared without even saying good-bye.

14

The moment he crossed the threshold of my studio, Black-Sea Islander announced: "I have a matter of global significance to discuss with you."

"Not really?"

Seregin, right?"

"Yes, he left just a short while ago."

"Splendid! He is a student of semantics, right?"

"Let me explain. You have a graduate student named

"Yes. In a year or so he'll be defending his dissertation."

"Excellent. But it wouldn't hurt you to learn a few pertinent facts about you protégé."

"What sort of facts?"

"He's a shady character."

"Careful, I don't like to hear my friends slandered."

"I understand. But not only is he a shady character—he's a fool besides. He's gullible. Imagine, he let himself be talked into believing something utterly preposterous: that a book seller named Spiridonov, is a visitor from space, no less, an emissary from extraterrestrial reason. Isn't that funny?"

"It's no laughing matter. Who, in fact, is he?"

"Why he's my ward. I got him from a children's home, taught him languages, sciences, good manners. But no sooner than he finished school, did he become ill, fancying himself to be an emissary from some outer space civilization. He has an extraordinarily powerful imagination, phenomenal powers of telepathy and clairvoyance. Besides that, he has immense abilities to talk himself and others into believing in all this nonsense."

"Haven't you tried to exploit those immense abilities?"

"Why so blunt and unfair? Yes, I consult him on occasion. I've brought him up, after all. But, let's get back to your graduate student. He seems to be turning Seryozha against me. I won't stand for that."

"But what do you want me to do about it?"

"I want you to make him stop it."

"He is, after all, a graduate student, not a schoolboy. In one more year he'll be getting his Ph.D. How can I interfere?"

"Then I'll be obliged to appeal to the press for protection. I have an international reputation. I think neither you nor your protégé would welcome the publicity."

Then, a moment later, he reverted to his former, more polite tone.

"I'm really sorry. Only truly global circumstances have obliged me to pry you away from your affairs. I hope that you'll explain to your gullible graduate student that he's mistaken. Seryozha was born of earthly parents. Earthly, understand?"

"What was it that gave him the idea?"

"I'll be completely frank with you," he said, "although I don't know whether you deserve my frankness. The environment in my home had a profound effect on Seryozha's consciousness. The weird atmosphere, the mental contacts with space and the cosmos. And, of course, there were my books, which he was crazy about when he was in school."

Suddenly he got up from his chair. "Excuse me, I must run. I'm leaving in hopes that you will make things clear to your graduate student. My adopted son, Seryozha, is ill. To use the words of a poet, 'marvelously ill.' His illness permits him to perform near miracles. But it's an illness, nevertheless. Do warn him, please. I'll give you a call."

15

As I was telling Seregin about Black-Sea Islander's visit, I closely watched the expression on his face. It was changing, becoming gloomy, until the moment when he suddenly burst out laughing.

"And you believed him?" he asked. "You believed him?"

"I'd much rather not believe him. Much rather! But you must agree that, after all, common sense is on his side. I struggled with myself the whole time. I was in doubt even when the picture, played that preposterous game of hide-and-seek with my logic. But he explained everything."

"So, he explained everything. Did he also explain why he's having an artistic crisis now?"

"No, he didn't mention the crisis. But you must agree that all creative people hit a block every once in a while."

"I grant you that. Let's say you're right about the crisis, and that Seryozha has talked himself into believing he's an emissary from space. But where did he acquire such an enormous amount of knowledge? Where did he learn all those things which our experience and modern science know nothing about? Is he a clever magician, or a sort of clairvoyant or hypnotist?"

"At any rate, that's easier to believe than that emissary stuff. Besides, what motive would Black-Sea Islander have for keeping the truth from us?"

"The simplest motive in the world—Seryozha's a gold mine for him, a real gold mine."

"Suppose he is? It's a thousand times easier to believe that Seryozha is a clairvoyant and a telepathist, than to believe that he's from another planet. Why, the trip alone would take thousands of light years. . . ."

"Perhaps we should discuss something else. How are things with your police lieutenant?"

"Avdeichev? Everything's fine. The neuropathologist ordered him to take a vacation and rest somewhere out in the country. And he advised him not to take any science-fiction novels along. Especially the kind that affect the nerves. I saw the lieutenant yesterday when he came to say good-bye. You ought to take a lesson from that lieutenant and get away from it all."

Seregin actually took my advice and went off to the Pushkin Mountains with Seryozha. Seryozha had been dying to go to the Pushkin Mountains, and this was his chance. But that evening my graduate student left without giving any indication whatsoever that he was upset."

I put on my overcoat and went out in the street. Something drew me in the direction of the bookstore on Bolshoi Avenue. There was quite a crowd in the bookstore at that hour. I stopped not far from the cash register in the corner and looked around. Seryozha, as usual, was at his place behind the counter. He had shaved his beard and his mustache, and now he resembled neither Dickens nor Chekhov. He looked like an ordinary, modern young man from an educated family. I stared at him as though hoping to catch a glimpse, in his now ordinary appearance, of something that did not have its origins on our planet. But something hindered me.

My perception lacked sharpness, as it does after a sleepless night, when one looks out the window and tries to piece the world back together.

He raised his head and saw me. At that same moment his appearance merged with the impression of him that I had before the chat with Islander. It was as though everything ordinary and familiar had vanished with the wind. He was no longer Seryozha Spiridonov, but that other one, the emissary from the unknown.

16

As he had promised, Black-Sea Islander phoned me one day. "Can you tell me where Seryozha is now?" he asked.

"I know—in the Pushkin mountains, with his friend, my graduate student. I received a rather nice card from him."

"But why the Pushkin mountains? Why so far?"

"It's a beautiful spot, linked with the memory of a great poet."

"Damn your platitudes! Don't you understand? They're taking my son away from me. Put yourself in my place."

"I don't write science fiction."

"But your own job is also out of the ordinary. You are attempting to separate man from his language and look at what comes of it. What is semantics? The study of communication with the aid of signs. My Seryozha, by blending his own self with that of his interlocutor, can get along without signs, without the aid of language. His telepathic possibilities are limitless. Yes, he's a phenomenon, An *earthly* phenomenon, *earthly,* but extraordinary. Neither time nor space exists for him. Perhaps Seryozha really is in contact with another civilization. But he is an *earthling.* I won't concede on that point! I raised him! Here, on earth, in this city! And now your graduate student has taken him off to the Pushkin mountains. And that was no mere accident."

"I don't quite understand," I interrupted him, "what danger the Pushkin Mountains could possibly represent. . . ."

"He's too impressionable! And besides. . . . No, I can't tell you everything. There are some things I must keep to myself . . . for the time being. Good-bye!" And he hung up the receiver.

17

The letter from Seregin was like a fragment of a dream. Valya wrote about his friend Seryozha in a manner so vague and mysterious that only with great effort was I able to get through the sea of words to the main idea, to the strange, alien, unearthly logic which once again started to play games with Seregin and, through him, with me as well.

According to my graduate student, Seryozha lamented the fact that he was too late. He absolutely had to meet the great poet Alexander Pushkin, but because of a tiny error in calculations a whole era replaced another here on earth, and now, alas, it was too late.

Why did he have to meet Pushkin? Why not Lamarck, or Einstein? Seryozha explained it to his friend Valya, and Valya was explaining it to me now, devoting fully three pages of this lengthy letter to it. The pages were explaining something that I was not capable of comprehending. I exerted all my mental powers to understand the implications of the phenomenon which Valya was describing to me. He wrote that Pushkin was the voice of rivers and forests, and through him nature herself spoke with us. I accepted that as a poetic expression, a metaphor, but Seryozha took it literally. What amazed me most was that the graduate student had learned to think exactly like his amazing friend.

But let's get back to the letter which was lying in front of me on my desk, beckoning me to the realm of vague, undeciphered thoughts not translated into the language of our earthly logic. There were obvious omissions in the letter. Valya could not or did not want to say everything that uncompromising clairty of thought would require.

"What would you have talked about with Pushkin, had you not been one hundred and thirty years late?"

Seryozha didn't answer my question. Then I told him that Pushkin, in spite of his towering intellect, was not ready for a conversation with an emissary from another civilization. He had lived in the first half of the nineteenth century, when there were no space ships and the madness of nuclear energy had not yet disturbed the peace.

Seryozha remained silent, as though he had not heard my remark. Yes, there was a stone wall between us, and I had already begun to regret that I had come here with him. Seryozha had a habit of taking walks with me, but being completely absorbed in himself most of the time. Every now and then he would suddenly prick up his ears as if to hear something that was inaudible to me, but which had reached his hypersensitive ears.

On that day which I'm telling you about we went out for a walk. Seryozha looked around as though he had been here at some previous time. Softly and pensively he repeated:

> It was late. They sky grew dark.
> The waters rushed. A beetle chirped.*

After we had returned he suddenly asked me, "Would you like to experience it?"

"What?" I asked.

A grin played on his face. "Don't ask. Do you want to?"

"I want to," I answered softly.

And then I suddenly felt I was a riverbank and a birch grove, and Pushkin was there beside me. I heard his footsteps and his voice reciting more lines from *Eugene Onegin*:

> On she walked. And suddenly before her
> From a hill she sees the manor house,
> The village, the grove beneath the hill,
> The park above the shining river.

He was there, and the seconds flowed like water. His footsteps on the path and the touch of his gentle hand on the trunk of the birch tree—I no longer thought about who I was—myself, a grove or the poet's words. Then, suddenly, it was all over.

---

* Translator's note: From *Eugene Onegin*, Chapter VII, XV.

"Did you hear him?" Seryozha asked softly.

"I heard him."

"But that was the grove talking."

"Isn't it all the same?" I asked.

Each time our conversation turned to Pushkin, Seryozha would speak in a whisper, as though the poet were around and could hear what was being said about him. The sensation that the distant past was right there beside us thrilled me, like the ocean depths, and I plumbed the depths of that amazing condition, never reaching the bottom. All around me and inside me, time surged back and forth like the rise and fall of the sea. It was a mystery, and a solution to it flashed through my mind, briefly illuminating that dark unknown, but it was only a suggestion, of which I could not be certain.

Man possesses a memory which preserves his past life and experience. Seryozha is not a man in our sense. He is the product of another evolutionary process, another unearthly, unknown biosphere. Evolution had given him the mysterious and wondrous ability to fathom the waves of time. I questioned Seryozha, trying to catch at least a glimpse of his unusual vision, but each time he would joke and laugh and end up by insisting that all poets and artists are endowed with that gift. I would remind him that our dialogue had begun, and that in the entire history of the earth there was, perhaps, no more significant conversation than ours. Then he would laugh even louder and would act as silly as a school boy during recess. No one around would guess that the man whom I called Seryozha was no less worthy of attention than any famous actor or some other celebrity. Everyone considered him the most ordinary guy in the world, especially the tourists who flock to the Pushkin Mountains.

Yet, even such a being as Seryozha, who was seemingly quite free of our earthly shortcomings, was not without certain human feelings. One day, unable to resist the temptation to show off, he committed a really frivolous act, not at all worthy of the great mission which he was sent here to fulfill. He caught sight of a rather plump woman tourist who was lolling around, bored to tears, and he turned her into a cloud. He let her float above the fields and the river for a little while and then safely brought her back to earth as though by parachute. It was impossible to hide the fact from observant eyes, especially since the cloud was shaped exactly like a rather fat woman. At first she was timid about the whole thing, but, encouraged by the lively interest in her, she finally admitted that the cloud had been herself. Now we're going to have to get out of here as fast as possible to avoid questions which would be difficult to answer.

18

I hardly finished reading the letter from my graduate student, when the telephone rang. This time Black-Sea Islander's voice was terribly gentle and even lyrical. A wave of warmth and tenderness gushed out at me from the receiver.

"Dear colleague," he addressed me.

"Pardon me," I interrupted him, "I don't write science-fiction novels and I never intend to. . . ."

"Dear colleague," he repeated, "I didn't always write novels, either, and I won't be writing them forever. Right now I'm gathering material for a short story on a subject related to the theory of sign systems, semantics. I'm counting on your kind assistance—a very modest amount of help, a little bit of consultation."

"But you have a consultant."

"Who?"

"Seryozha."

"That ignoramus? That salesman who practices sorcery and spreads all sorts of superstition and rumors. And in our century! Sooner or later the authorities will catch up with him. Or don't you think so?"

Instead of replying, I hung up the receiver. The phone rang again, and then again, but I didn't answer it. Nevertheless, his persistence and aggressiveness were more than I could withstand, and I finally accepted this unseeming role and began to advise this man, even though he did not inspire any sympathy in me. I didn't have the strength of character to refuse, and perhaps I was tempted by a feeling that somehow I had to replace Seryozha, the most extraordinary of all the advisers and consultants who ever lived on earth.

In gratitude, Black-Sea Islander made me a gift of all the books he had written. And here I sit reading them, trying to find traces of Seryozha's assistance. Alas, all those numerous novels and stories did not serve as a bridge connecting earthly reality with that realm which was preserved in Seryozha's memory. What was wrong? I couldn't explain it to myself, and I'm unable to explain it to you.

It can't be said that Islander made no effort to present and explain in earthly terms things that were unusual and beyond our ordinary frame of reference. He always directed his thoughts toward places far beyond the bounds of our solar system, but in his heart, in all his frames of reference he remained on earth, in his comfortable apartment with its ordinary, homey atmosphere. In short, Black-Sea Islander had too much of the glib writer in him, and not enough of the imaginative writer. The traditional and, in many ways, antiquated method of the naive, picaresque novel was incapable of grasping and conveying the complex essence of Seryozha's mature experience, through which the biosphere and history of some mysterious planet was attempting to speak to us.

Black-Sea Islander's books reminded me of a trap from which the prey had escaped without touching the bait. Annoyed, I closed the books and put them away on a shelf.

Nevertheless, the writer appreciated the difference between me and Seryozha, and would let me feel it from time to time. He didn't even hesitate to say, "If only you were from there, too."

"From where?" I asked.

"You know—there, where Seryozha came from."

"Did he really come from somewhere else? Didn't you get him from an orphanage?"

"Yes, yes," he would nod his head in agreement. "I only meant it in a metaphorical sense."

He would sit beside me, listening half-heartedly. I would be explaining something to him, an ideogram for example. On a sheet of paper I drew a container with water pouring from it—a sample ideogram, which illustrated the property of coolness. Yes, there was a time on the earth when people sought information that was too graphic and concrete, for they were as yet unable to separate conception, ideas from the shapes that things assumed, from the very form of things. I would speak in accordance with the logic of that fascinating discipline to which I had devoted many years. But the writer didn't listen well. His thoughts kept returning to Seryozha.

"I'll expose him," grumbled the venerable visionary. "He's a cheap charlatan. Sorcery is forbidden as a dangerous remnant of the past."

"I've never noticed anything in the laws about sorcery," I said. "The laws have overlooked sorcery."

"What about superstition?"

"Everything he does is on a strictly scientific basis, experience that he brought down here to us on earth!"

"Typical pseudoscience, the twin sister of telepathy."

"There's nothing about pseudoscience in the laws, either."

"We're talking about sorcery. I'll put a stop to it. I'll expose him through the press."

I tried to reason with him, to get him off the subject, to interest him in my favorite science, the history of signs. I told him all about the ancient Egyptian cuneiform alphabet, but he wasn't listening.

"I'm a man of principles," he said, "and my materialistic philosophy won't let me accept this superstition that he is spreading around here."

"But earlier," I argued, "when Seryozha collaborated with you, your philosophy permitted you to ignore his strangeness."

"That was my mistake, and now I must correct it."

"What do you intend to do?"

"To put a stop to it. It's unthinkable that an ignorant person should be allowed to sell books. We must put a stop to every kind of sorcery immediately."

"But the facts," I asked, "where are your facts?"

"Facts? As many as you want. I've heard rumors that

in the Pushkin Mountains he permitted himself to play a suspicious game with common sense. Imagine, an elderly tourist, a teacher of English . . . Yes, he compromised her morals."

19

Seregin was upset about something. He was sitting opposite me by the window, nervously smoking, obviously worried by something.

"What's wrong?" I asked. "Seryozha?"

"He's ill, and it's a strange disease. He's changed somehow, put on weight, and he seems shorter. He's changed so much that he can't report to work."

"Is he that sick?"

"On the contrary, he feels great, but is changing, he's becoming a completely different person. They do not even consider it an illness and won't give him sick leave or put him in a hospital. They won't give him the help he needs."

"Exactly what happened?"

"Have you ever seen a portrait of the famous French writer Guy de Maupassant?"

"Of course!"

"Well, now he could pass for Maupassant's double—the black moustache, the deep voice, the ruddy complexion. Do you understand? Now he is Maupassant."

"How can it be?" I asked.

"I don't know. That's what I came to talk to you about."

"But Seryozha himself—does he have any explanation for it?"

"Seryozha? Well, there's no Seryozha around anymore. There's only Guy de Maupassant, the famous French writer."

"Does he imagine himself to be Maupassant?"

"He doesn't imagine it—he has become him. He's fully convinced that he's living in the nineteenth century. I simply don't know what to do. Worst of all, you can't explain anything to anybody."

"Have you tried to impress on him the fact that he's not Maupassant, that it's a mistake, a misunderstanding?"

"I've tried. It doesn't work. Would you believe me if I tried to make you believe that you're not yourself, but somebody else?"

"But I'm not somebody else. I'm myself."

"Precisely. He, too, has no reason to think that he's not he, but Maupassant. Even the mirror confirms it. Sometimes even I think that he's Maupassant, that the course of time has somehow shifted, with Seryozha winding up in the nineteenth century, and Maupassant turning up here in his place. The whole thing is confusing and illogical, even a worse mess than that business with the picture that kept appearing and disappearing. Sometimes I think Seryozha is experimenting, seeking ways to establish contact with earthly humanity, and this is why he's playing games with you and me."

"Did he ever do it with anyone else?"

"Yes, once. Black-Sea Islander sent him off to a sanitorium run especially for scientists and philosophers. And he couldn't think of anything better to do, so he upped and turned into Spinoza."

"Why Spinoza? For that matter, why Maupassant? Why Dickens? Why not Victor Hugo or Alexander Dumas or Turgenev or Flaubert?"

"I don't know. I don't know anything. All I know is that I do not know what's going to happen next and I am worried about it. What is going to happen next?"

I couldn't find the answer to that. However, life itself provided the answer.

Little by little everyone became accustomed to Guy de Maupassant, the famous French writer. It was true, however, that most people assumed that it was merely a chance resemblance, a gift from forgetful nature.

This went on for no more than two weeks. Then the famous French writer disappeared, returned to his own century, and Seryozha turned up in his place. My graduate student immediately informed me of this by telephone. Later that day he came over to my place, and filled me in on the details.

"Maupassant went to the bathroom to take a shower. He was gone about twenty minutes, then forty. I started to worry, and looked in on him. Instead of Maupassant, I saw Seryozha standing there, rubbing his back with a Turkish towel.

" 'Where's Maupassant?' I asked him. 'What do you mean?' said Seryozha in amazement. 'He's at home, in France, in nineteenth century France.' He winked at me ironically."

"What does he plan to do now?" I asked.

"How should I know? Maupassant is gone."

"I'm not asking about Maupassant. Tell me about Seryozha."

"What's there to tell? He took a shower, shaved, and went to work."

That was all I could learn from my graduate student. I shrugged my shoulders and asked him, "And how's your dissertation coming along?"

"I won't let you down. But if I am held up a little bit, there is a valid excuse,"

"What's that?"

"Guy de Maupassant. He took up a lot of my time. Why don't you call on him at the bookstore?"

The next morning I dropped by the bookstore on Bolshoi Avenue. Seryozha was at his usual place.

"Nothing much, a one-volume edition of Maupassant,

"Hello," I said.

"Hi!"

"Any new books?"

an excellent edition, with illustrations by Rudakov and a portrait of the author on parchment. Would you like to take a look at it?"

"Yes, let me see it."

He took the book off the shelf, opened it and showed me the portrait. I suddenly felt faint. It was Guy de Maupassant, and yet it wasn't because of a subtle resemblance to

Seryozha. I glanced at the portrait again, and it seemed that the famous writer was winking at me. "That's not Maupassant," I said.

"You think not?" Seryozha closed the book and put it back on the shelf.

"You ought to stop playing your tricks and setle down," I said.

"You think so?"

"Disgraceful!" I said, slamming the door as I left the bookshop.

20

Seregin was having a bad time with his dissertation. The excerpt that he brought in was appalling. Instead of concentrating on his topic dealing with the theory of signs, he had written about Planet N. As I was reading the excerpt I kept imagining the expression on the faces of the dissertation committee members and their comments, which would begin something like: "It seems that because of a mistake on the part of the typist or the candidate himself, an excerpt from a science-fiction novel somehow found its way into the dissertion. . . ."

"This is not a scholarly piece of work," I told Seregin.

"Then what is it?"

"It's fantasy, fiction, a fable."

"It's based on proven facts."

"Who proved them? Police Lieutenant Avdeichev? That lady whom Seryozha supposedly turned into a cloud? Who would believe you?"

"They'll believe Seryozha, not me."

"All right, suppose they will, contrary to all laws of common sense. What does this manuscript have to do with you and your dissertation?"

"By means of my dissertation Seryozha wants to make contact with human civilization and begin, at last, a dialogue between earthlings and other-planetary beings. It's not my idea, it's Seryozha's."

"But why? Certainly not to help you earn your degree. If he's really been sent here from another world, then even making you a full member of the Academy is hardly sufficient reward."

"You seem to be laughing."

"I would like to follow Spinoza's advice: Don't laugh, don't cry, simply understand. But I can't. What are you trying to do—turn your dissertation defence into an international event? Have you thought of the consequences?"

"I have. And I've said 'no' a hundred times. But Seryozha insists."

"I don't understand either one of you. You'll be accused of being a sensationalist."

"Oh, for goodness' sake, it's not a sensation is that? It's an event. It's a revolution in science, an exchange of information, unprecedented in the history of this planet."

"We're not living in a world of miracles, but in a world of ordinary facts. No member of the academic council is prepared to accept this strange phenomenon. You'll be accused of a pseudoscientific plot, and they'll send your Seryozha off for an examination. Some of them will say that he is a telepathist with a unique psychic make-up, and others will say that he's a charlatan and a magician."

"But you know perfectly well that he's not a charlatan or a magician or even a telepathist."

"That's just the point—I don't know. He doesn't even know himself. He's carrying on in the most scandalous way."

"What do you mean?"

"Everything. First he helped Black-Sea Islander to concoct his science-fiction novels, and now he's helping you write your dissertation. No, I can't allow this."

"I can't permit this whole dubious game with common sense to become a part of your dissertation."

"Please give me a little more time," asked Seregin.

"All right," I said. "You have a week. I hope you'll weigh all the pros and cons and renounce your strange intention."

A week passed. It was a week of doubts, sleeplessness, and conflicts with myself. I had great faith in Seregin's abilities, in his enthusiasm and energy, in the originality of his thinking processes. But there is a limit to everything. Common sense wouldn't let me consent to this risky and awkward experiment.

Even if his wondrous theory is genuine, Seregin received it as a gift from the future too easily and casually. Morally he had no right to accept that gift from fate. Neither Lobachevsky nor Einstein found his wondrous theory on the sidewalk, the way one finds an abandoned purse. If they had, they would have taken it back to the lost and found. But Seregin wanted to take advantage of his find. And I cannot, I don't have the moral right to condone that.

21

I found Seryozha busy selling books, as always.

"I have to talk with you," I said.

"Right now I'm at work," he said coldly. "I'm not supposed to get involved in private conversations."

"Fine. I'll wait for you on the square." I had to wait about an hour. Seryozha came up quietly and sat down beside me. His face no longer seemed severe and distant, but had assumed a good-hearted, ordinary expression.

"What are you up to?" I asked him, "trying to help my grad student write his dissertation?"

"Why shouldn't I?" asked Seryozha and grinned.

"Unfortunately, he wants to turn the defense of his dissertation into an international event."

"It's not he who wants it," Seryozha corrected me. "I do."

"But why?"

"I can't simply go to the Academy of Sciences or some

newspaper office and say that I've come to share my experience with mankind."

"Exactly what's stopping you? If you have something to say to mankind, then that's precisely where you ought to go."

"I would go there, but it's sort of awkward. The noise! The publicity! I hate that sort of thing. Press photographers drive me crazy."

"You can't avoid it," I said.

"I'm trying to. Press photographers don't attend dissertation defenses."

"But what about your mission?"

"That's the whole point. As it is I've been putting off my dialogue with humanity. I can't drag this thing out much longer. Time keeps on moving for us the same way it does for you. Besides that, there's something else I like about all this."

"What's that?"

"It's so down-to-earth, so simple. What could be less pretentious than a dissertation defense? On the other hand, the idea is not at all commonplace: contact between two civilizations, an earthly one and a nonearthly one. And it's not merely a hypothesis—it's a fact."

"A fact? But where? What kind of a fact?"

"Myself. Isn't that fact enough for you?"

"My own objections aren't the only ones to be considered. Other members of the Academic Council will be there. I'm sure there will be complications."

"I'll be there to make everything go smoothly."

"With your telepathy and hypnotism?"

"With bare facts that I'll reveal to them right there on the spot. They'll understand who I am, where I'm from and why I'm here."

"I think some of them won't like it at all."

"Seryozha stood up. "Excuse me, my lunch hour's almost up. If you don't mind, I'll drop back by to see you. We'll continue our conversation later."

We did continue the conversation.

"I know," said Seryozha quietly, "that you don't believe I'm from there."

"You're right, I don't believe it."

"Why?"

"Life is a rare phenomenon in the universe, don't you agree? And common sense is even rarer. How did you get here?"

"You'll find that out as soon as your grad student finishes his dissertation. I can't answer that particular question until then. But you can ask me other questions."

"Tell me something about your civilization."

"What's there to tell? You know practically all there is to know about it from science-fiction novels. For example, we learned how to control gravity a long time ago, when Earth was still in the Paleolithic era. And we populated the neighboring planets, after we created a biosphere for them and improved the climate. We also learned how to slow down time. We established contact with several other civilizations. To do that we had to reshape time and space. It wasn't easy." He covered his mouth to conceal a yawn.

"All of this that I'm telling you is so old that it even bores me. You look like you're really eating it up. We also invented a machine that re-creates existence and things. But that's not new either. You see me right here in front of you, don't you? But hasn't it occurred to you that maybe I'm not here, that maybe I'm back there, where I came from? This is only my image recreating itself. I don't think your science-fiction writers have ever described this sort of thing. And then, just between you and me, I don't look anything at all like that Seryozha who sells books. You only see me that way."

"Then what do you really look like?" I asked.

"Maybe I'm a monster with an antler for a nose. Or maybe I'm a minotaur. It's no trouble at all for me to assume any appearance I want. It pleases me to assume the likeness of people who have long been dead. I've been told that's indiscreet. But would I be more discreet if suddenly I started looking like you? Resemblance to any living person hurts people's feelings, wounds their pride, for each and everyone of you thinks he's unique.

"What else can I tell you? You see, the civilization which sent me here has reached the stage when each of us is a god who creates himself and his whole environment. That's why I am so fascinated by the commonplace and wish to experience it. The ordinary way of life has been preserved here on earth as nowhere else. It was depicted by Chekhov, the most profound and the most modest of all human writers. I owe him a great debt for what he has taught me."

"How did you manage to make contact with Chekhov?"

"Quite simply. I read everything he wrote. I learned that the commonplace is actually a great thing. In making gods out of us, our civilization deprived us of. . . ."

"Of what?"

"A great deal. But mainly simplicity. I'm a little tired of being a god. I'd like to live in a little less ingenious world, where people haven't yet learned to reshape time and space, to codify things and organisms, to create things that are unnecessary or even necessary, including themselves. I know that this is merely a passing weakness, a spiritual lapse, possibly even a mistake. I'll correct my mistake during your student's dissertation defense. And then I'll return to my own world. I'll encode myself and send myself off the way you send a telegram." Seryozha looked at me sadly, as though he had already parted with earth. "Well, do you believe it now or not?"

"Yes, I do. I think I do. But not enough to let this get into Seregin's dissertation."

That was not the end of our rather lengthy conversation. Seryozha dropped in on me several more times. He tried to convince me, pleaded with me, added more details of the ingenious world of his civilization and each time he always got around to his favorite subject.

"So then you simply don't have it at all—the ordinary, the commonplace, I mean?" I asked him.

"We used to have it, but then it ended. I don't remember in what century that happened."

"But how do you get along without it? I can't quite picture it. You mean, people on your planet do not acquire habits, never get used to anything?"

"Everything is too mobile, too transient to become familiar or a habit. The main thing is that everyone can do anything he wants. Everyone is a god."

"A god?"

"Not really a god, but sort of like one."

"Doesn't it ever get boring?"

"Boring? I'm not sure I know what this word means,"

"How should I explain boredom to you? That's the sort of feeling you have when it seems like you're about a thousand years old and you've seen everything there is to see."

"No, I've never had that feeling. On the contrary, it has always seemed to me that I was just born, although I've been living for. . . . That's right! Tomorrow I'll be three."

"Three years old?"

"Not three, a thousand and three. But on my passport I put down a more reasonable age. I didn't want to frighten the girl who might one day agree to marry me. But then she won't probably. Who'd want to marry a minotaur?"

"Are you a minotaur?"

"Let's not get into that. But I do like mythology. I'm sorry I missed the ancient Greeks. I was about three thousand years too late. However, it's not so bad here with you people. I want to live in a less ingenious world, where man hasn't yet been relieved of all his cares. Life isn't easy, especially for a minotaur."

"Why?"

"I'm half earthling, half other-worldling. I have to carry around two worlds, two value systems in me. Do you think that's easy?"

"I don't imagine so."

Seryozha suddenly gave me a long inquiring look and asked, "Do you deserve my frankness?"

"I'm not the one to ask this question."

"The problem is that Seregin is trying to get me to exchange fates with him."

"What do you mean? I don't understand."

"He wants me to stay here, and he wants me to encode him and send him to my world."

"Is that ethical?"

"What do you think?"

"I don't think it is. You have a family back there. Besides, if he plans to disappear for a long time, if not forever, then why should he worry about his dissertation? Back there it probably doesn't make the least bit of difference whether he's a Ph.D. or an ordinary mortal."

"It's much more complicated than you think. He's got his pride."

"Are you prepared to change places with him or not?"

"I haven't decided yet. But, let's get back to the dissertation—will you sponsor it?"

"No," I answered, "let him complete his dissertation for another advisor I cannot sponsor the changed subject."

22

A minotaur is one of those creatures from Cretan mythology. It is half-man, half-bull whom, according to ancient legend, King Minos locked up in a labyrinth built by the Athenian Daedalus. But now reality itself had created a labyrinth for me, one which confounded me and my logic, my innate common sense. The only way out of the labyrinth was to remain faithful to the ethics of scholarship and to relinquish sponsorship of Seregin's dissertation. Did I believe that Seryozha was an emissary from some unknown yet actual world that was infinitely far away? I believed it, and yet I didn't believe it.

I broke off all contact with my student Seregin. I tried to forget about everything that had preoccupied me during that strange year. And when I would walk past the bookstore on Bolshoi Avenue, my curiosity about the unknown urged me to come in, but each time I forced myself to walk on.

Engrossed in my work, I was gradually forgetting the strange and mysterious events which had played games with me. But a notice I chanced to see on the forth page of the Leningrad *Evening News* suddenly dragged me back into that labyrinth from which I had only recently escaped.

"On May 28," I read, "in the Faculty of Philosophy of Leningrad University, V. V. Seregin will defend his doctoral dissertation *Cosmic Liguistics*. Visiting Professor Minotaur is the official opponent."

When I finished reading this notice, I experienced the same feeling that I had when I saw my picture in the science-fiction novel. "I must see Seryozha" I thought to myself. And at that very moment I did see him. He was sitting behind a folding table, selling books and lottery tickets.

"Are you coming to the defense?" asked Seryozha. He did not seem to be surprised to see me.

"No, I'm not coming."

"Then, tomorrow night at eight, turn on your television set without fail."

Exactly at eight, I turned on the television set. They were showing an everyday scene from academic life—a defense of a doctoral dissertation. My former student, Seregin, was standing on the rostrum, addressing the members of the Academic Council with quiet confidence:

"Their logic, their view of the world is consistent with their milieu. A myth? To some extent it is, but it is a myth created not by imagination, by fantasy, by control over the laws of nature. My esteemed opponent, Professor Minotaur, has given me permission to show some film strips which were brought here to Earth. . . . Projectionist, please turn out the lights."

And at that moment the face of a woman looking into a hand mirror appeared on the television screen. In the woman's hand, bound in a round frame, was a transparent lake with fish swimming on the bottom. Then there appeared a wall on which a painting was hanging. Inside the frame there was a living forest in which the trees, swept by a strong wind, were rustling.

Seregin continued: "My esteemed opponent, Professor Minotaur, will tell you about this amazing planet and its strange, magnificent civilization, so different from our own. And I shall limit myself to a brief summary of the subject of my dissertation, *Cosmic Linguistics.*"

Translated by THOM WATTS.